S0-AAC-930

Praise for

The Cape Cod Witch Series

"Graced with colorful watercolors evoking an olde New England, this children's romp is a sure bet for young readers who might occasionally prefer to imbibe their Harry Potter-style adventures closer to home."

- Vineyard Gazette, Martha's Vineyard

"It's a fast and fun read. . . . It's like *Sabrina the Teenage Witch* crossed with *Sarah Plain and Tall* – sort of. Earthy and homemade feeling, the writing and story read like local folklore but with contemporary characters. I can see why it is a hit with younger readers and I, too, liked it a lot."

- Ypulse Book Reviews

"ElsBeth could be a very influential figure in children's literature. . . . She's a strong witch with an enduring spirit who could tackle any number of problems. I can see many other magical characters being introduced in her tutelage. All the makings present for an exciting children's book series."

- Sabrina Williams, breenibooks.com

More Praise for

The Cape Cod Witch and the Pirates Treasure

"J Bean Palmer has penned an entertaining novel for young readers about the Cape's youngest witch, ElsBeth Amelia Thistle."

– Cape Cod Times

"*The Cape Cod Witch and the Pirate's Treasure*" is a well-written, faced-paced, and entertaining tale of mystery and adventure, with well-developed and likeable characters. It blends everyday situations at school and home with magic, witches, and fairies. . . . The colorful, childlike illustrations add much to the appeal of the book and may encourage even reluctant readers to pick it up."

– Sandwich Enterprise

"Fairies, witches, toads, pirates, and Indians make up the character-driven cast of *The Cape Cod Witch and the Pirate's Treasure*. . . . The cast is an interesting cross between magic and reality.

"ElsBeth sets an example for her classmates with her reverence of nature, encouraging them to consider how their actions affect creatures of the wild. This is an admirable quality to include in children's literature."

– breenibooks.com

The Cape Cod Witch and the Legend of the Pirate

Written by
J Bean Palmer

Illustrated by
Melanie Therrien

Holly Hill Press

Holly Hill Press
Post Office Box 36
East Sandwich, Massachusetts 02537

Layout and typesetting by Electronic Publishing Services
www.epubsinc.com

ISBN 978-0-578-01217-9

Copyright 2009 by J Bean Palmer
Artwork Copyright 2009 by Melanie Therrien
All Rights Reserved

Library of Congress Control Number: 2009923572

Published in the USA

March 2009

Educators and librarians can visit our website for teaching notes at
www.capecodlittlewitch.com

The Amazing Story
of ElsBeth Amelia Thistle,
Cape Cod's Youngest Witch

Follow along as she and her daring
friends attempt to rescue
a kidnapped Arabian Prince . . . .

And you, too, will come to know the
Legend of the Pirate!

Dedication

This book is dedicated to
Emelia "Shell" Bean and little Maddie,

To the eldest Bean -
thank you for believing in all of us,

And to all the teachers who inspire,
and all the children who inspire us.

This story is for you.

TABLE OF CONTENTS

Cape Cod Massachusetts
Home of ElsBeth Amelia Thistle,
Cape Cod's Youngest Witch

Chapter I
MS. FINCH STRIKES AGAIN

It is present day Cape Cod, Massachusetts. Somewhere near the elbow. This is a place of old and powerful magic. But lately forces here have not been in balance. The area's oldest resident witch, Hannah Prudence Goodspell, though legendary throughout her several centuries practicing white magic, is now . . . well, to put it bluntly . . . losing it.

Strange and disturbing things have been happening in the quiet seaside settlement.

Let's take a closer look in on the quaint village and its unusual inhabitants to see if we can figure out what is going on.

Perched on her wooden seat in the third row of the narrow classroom, the youngest witch on Cape Cod, ElsBeth Amelia Thistle, was completely out-of-her-head wild with excitement. What an adventure they were going to have! The whole class was going on a field trip. All the way from the Cape to Boston. Beantown itself, home of the greatest baseball, football, basketball and hockey teams ever. At least that is what her pesky classmate, Robert Hillman-Jones, always said.

ElsBeth, being a bona fide witch, didn't really like to pay much attention to ordinary boys. But Hillman-Jones was utterly convincing when he spoke about local sports. The fellow second grader seemed unshakably certain that Boston was a sports town above all others.

ElsBeth was a little concerned about the upcoming trip, however. Her grandmother, normally completely supportive of ElsBeth's interests, had been reluctant for the little witch to go.

"Too many ghosts and ghouls around that town. Mean spirited, most of them," the older witch would add each time this subject was discussed. And to make matters worse, it had become difficult to have a serious discussion with her grandmother when she was so preoccupied by all the happenings around town lately.

And now that ElsBeth was almost through second grade, she was taking herself and her school life pretty seriously indeed. After all, how many witches made it through a whole year with Ms. Finch as their teacher? Well, almost made it.

The only time this entire school year that Ms. Finch had been at all pleasant had been on Halloween, when ElsBeth and her good friend Johnny Twofeathers had rescued Robert Hillman-Jones and several of the other second grade boys from the notorious pirate, Billy Bowlegs, and some nasty treasure hunters cleverly disguised as bird watchers. Ms. Finch had even given the children candy then. "Why couldn't it always be Halloween?" ElsBeth wondered philosophically.

But that was a long time ago. Now it was May. And though all of Cape Cod was green and alive and fresh with spring, Ms. Finch was her same, mean, old, stuffy self.

These thoughts were running through the little witch's mind while she was daydreaming during long division class.

"Ms. Thistle . . . Ms. Thistle . . . MS. THISTLE!!"

ElsBeth looked up, horrified to see a red-faced Finch leaning over her.

"I SAID, 'What is the quotient of 21 and 7?'"

"Quotient, quotient?" ElsBeth's mind raced. What was a quotient again? Oh no! ElsBeth had totally forgotten what a quotient was.

The little witch sat hard on her hands so that she didn't inadvertently cast a "holding spell" on Ms. Finch, even though it would have given ElsBeth time to look up what a quotient was. The young witch was *definitely* not allowed to use magic at school.

ElsBeth decided that honesty was her only hope. It was better than making up an answer, or guessing – especially wrongly.

"A quotient . . . I don't remember what a quotient is," the young witch stuttered.

Oh no! ElsBeth had just broken at least three Finch rules:

> One – She didn't know the answer.
>
> Two – She hadn't been paying attention.
>
> And Three – She forgot to end her statement with, "I'm sorry, Ms. Finch."

Boy, was she in for it now.

"Detention, Ms. Thistle – you'll stay after school for the rest of the week. You lack discipline, young lady! And I'm just the one to fix that," the teacher added with a superior sneer.

Ms. Finch walked away with a pleased look on her prunish face. She *loved* any excuse to give ElsBeth detention. Something about that girl just annoyed the teacher to no end. And ElsBeth's latest crime was worthy of punishment for the whole week. The stick-thin Ms. Finch rubbed her hands together in delight.

ElsBeth began to be seriously worried. She was already behind in her magic lessons at home. A whole week of detention would make it worse. How would she ever catch up?

The school day went on from there as it always did, and somehow, despite the horrifying beginning, ElsBeth managed to make it through with no further disasters.

When school was ending that afternoon and the children were packing up and heading out, her good friend Veronica stopped and said, "ElsBeth, you've got to get it together. Daydreaming in math class is just asking for trouble. You don't want detention next week. Four Seas Ice Cream parlour in Centerville is opening for the season, and *everyone* is going."

Veronica tossed her head. She had practiced this so that she looked just like that hip singer in the indie band Veronica's mother always went to see when they played the Vineyard. Veronica was always cool, and unlike ElsBeth, who tended to be a bit of a hot-head, Veronica had no worries as she headed out to a perfect Cape Cod afternoon.

When Johnny Twofeathers walked by next he gave ElsBeth a sympathetic nod. He had his own trials with the difficult teacher. The future Wampanoag chief didn't have to say anything to ElsBeth. ElsBeth always knew what her good friend was thinking. Even with just a nod in her direction, ElsBeth felt better.

Another classmate, Amy Clark, slipped by, her thick, blond banana curls hiding her face, except when she gave

ElsBeth an embarrassed glance and a timid smile of encouragement.

Nelson Hamm's ears turned red as he watched Amy longingly, following two steps behind the slight girl in pink. Nelson mumbled, "Well, it could have been worse," as he passed ElsBeth.

Robert Hillman-Jones came last. He swaggered past, kicked ElsBeth's desk and squeaked, mimicking ElsBeth's latest fiasco with Ms. Finch, "Oh quotient, quotient. What is a quotient?" He was laughing hard as he exited the classroom and burst out to the freedom of the school yard. *He* was going to have some fun.

ElsBeth frowned. She hung her head and slowly found her way back to the study hall to begin the rest of her long afternoon of detention with the Finch.

Sylvanas and Bartholomew

Chapter II
A BEFUDDLED WITCH AT SIX DRUID LANE

When ElsBeth got home that evening, her grandmother was unusually quiet. Normally the plump older witch would bound out of the garden, give ElsBeth a big hug, and ask her all about her day at school. Instead, Hannah Goodspell barely noticed her little granddaughter.

"What's up with Grandmother?" ElsBeth turned first to Sylvanas, the magical cat. Sylvanas didn't answer. He just looked back with his nose in the air, as if to say, "It is far beneath ME to pry" – which was a little ironic, as Sylvanas was probably the nosiest creature in the whole town, even perhaps in all of the Cape and Islands! He really was an impossible busybody.

ElsBeth, however, soon forgot her own concerns and the irksome Sylvanas when her grandmother cast the same spell three times in a row and nothing happened. ElsBeth realized something was really wrong. Hannah was one of the most respected witches in Massachusetts, and Massachusetts witches were the most respected witches in all the New World. If Hannah was this disturbed it must be serious. Was it more than just the fairies? They certainly could stir up more commotion than a barrel full of monkeys – smart, devilish monkeys at that.

ElsBeth decided to ask Bartholomew if he knew what was going on. Sylvanas clearly wasn't going to help in this matter.

Bartholomew, an extraordinarily large, bright green frog and formerly a handsome but incredibly vain Indian prince, could almost always be found relaxing in the garden. And he could almost always be counted on to listen to ElsBeth's difficulties. ElsBeth didn't really have many difficulties. But when she had them, she could count on Bartholomew for sound advice.

The little witch sat down in the minty medicinal herb section by the lemon verbena plants. Bartholomew was at eye level since he was settled comfortably on his ornately carved, green garden stool.

He turned his beautiful golden eyes to the young witch. "Don't worry, ElsBeth," he croaked. "Your grandmother is just a little anxious. There have been some new goings-on with the fairies. You just can't predict what they will get into next!"

ElsBeth thought there must be more to it than this. They'd had problems with the fairies since Halloween, when the little creatures had stirred up things at the pirate's cave. So trouble with them was nothing new, just one of those things a witch had to deal with on a daily basis. ElsBeth tried to question Bartholomew further, but no matter what ElsBeth asked, the magical frog just wouldn't say more. Bartholomew simply sat there serenely, humming a pleasant tune while dusk settled over the garden.

Why did ElsBeth feel there was much more to this than Bartholomew was letting on? Since she was a witch, she could sense things beneath the surface. But she couldn't for the life of her tell what *this* was all about.

There was nothing for it. She made up her mind she'd *really* have to talk with Sylvanas. *And* get him to answer. Right after dessert! Grandmother that morning, had said they might have maple custard at supper, and with the thought of this tempting treat, all else was instantly forgotten.

"Well, I'm sure it will be OK." ElsBeth jumped up, gave Bartholomew a quick hug, and went in to help with the meal.

As she stepped onto the porch, the heavenly scent of fairy cupcakes seeped into her senses. Double-double chocolate chip fairy-cream cupcakes were her all time favorite! Even better than maple custard. The little witch skipped happily inside.

Mathematics Lesson with
Professor Badinoff

Chapter III
MATHEMATICS HAS ITS USES

That evening after a delightful though unusually quiet dinner, Professor Badinoff, ElsBeth's familiar, spent a whole hour going over the basics of multiplication and division. For those who don't know, a witch's "familiar" is her special magical animal friend who helps and protects her, no matter what. And ElsBeth's familiar was a bat, Professor Badinoff.

The large bat was an extraordinary teacher. He had a way of explaining things, especially mathematics, that ElsBeth could understand with no difficulty. "Why couldn't Ms. Finch be more like Professor Badinoff?" ElsBeth thought. Then she started to giggle as she pictured Ms. Finch with pointy bat ears. ElsBeth slid to the floor and rolled around, shaking with belly laughs. That would be something!

Professor Badinoff cleared his throat. The large bat was an important and renowned intellect, after all. He didn't often have students rolling on the floor during math lessons. It was not proper!

"Yes, well, as I was saying . . ." the professor continued.

Badinoff pointed to the extensive collection of rubber tree frogs ElsBeth kept in her room. "ElsBeth, count out one hundred frogs, please."

ElsBeth busily counted the required number of amphibians and placed them in the center of the hooked rug by her bed.

The professor went to the slate chalkboard he always used for mathematics lessons. He wrote neatly, in ornate script, "*100 divided by 5 = ?*"

Then he had ElsBeth separate the one hundred frogs into five equal piles. ElsBeth placed the tree frogs by color as she liked the look of it that way. Green, brown, purple, orange and red frogs were now in neat rows.

"Now, ElsBeth, count how many frogs are in each group, please," the professor ordered in his serious, academic, teaching voice.

ElsBeth carefully counted the number of frogs in each group, her tongue sticking out of the side of her mouth with the effort of keeping track. "Twenty! There are exactly twenty in each."

"Precisely!" said Badinoff. Flapping his wing over the slate, he erased the question mark and wrote "*20*" in its place. "The quotient is twenty."

ElsBeth frowned, "What's a quotient?"

Badinoff smiled, his exceptional ears perking up. "Excellent question, ElsBeth. The word 'quotient' comes to us from Latin, an important language for magical beings, by the way.

"In Latin the word means 'how many times'. The basic idea is 'how many'. So if, for example, you had one hundred frogs and you wanted to split them up into five groups, so that you could have them jump out and surprise someone from all sides – you would have a nice total of twenty frogs in each group. Such knowledge comes in handy for cooking, spell making and in any serious battle – just to name a few uses off the top of my head," he added modestly.

"Wow! I would love to have a hundred frogs jumping out and surprising Ms. Finch when she's picking on me. Or at Robert Hillman-Jones when he's pulling my braids. I never knew mathematics could be so extremely useful. Thank you, Professor," she added respectfully.

The professor puffed out his chest and fluttered his wings a little at this sudden interest he had inspired in his young pupil. He was about to continue the lesson and get into his favorite Einstein equations when he had another look at ElsBeth's shining face. He saw that his young pupil had learned something important and that it was time to end off for now. So instead of diving into the next lesson the wonderful bat said, "Well . . . er . . . yes. I think that is enough for today. Well done, ElsBeth."

With a quick swoop of his wings he erased the board and took off out the window, looking for someone with whom he could debate some of Einstein's less understood theories – a favorite pastime of his when not gobbling up those tasty mosquitoes they have in New England!

A WITCH'S DREAMS BEGIN AGAIN

That night ElsBeth crawled happily into bed. She could see the silvery moon through her window. It seemed to be winking at her in a friendly fashion. The stars were twinkling, too. Her lids grew heavy and she soon dropped off to sleep. But it was a fitful sleep and full of dreams – oh, what dreams. . . .

"ElsBeth, save me!" Robert Hillman-Jones, dressed in his expensive Abercrombie & Fitch Kids clothes, was covered in muck, and he was stumbling down a dark tunnel. ElsBeth kept calling for him to stop, but her classmate went deeper and deeper into the darkness.

Something was after him, and ElsBeth couldn't catch up. She fell farther and farther behind. She was extremely tired. But she couldn't stop. She began to feel a cold presence, not of this Earth. Now something was chasing ElsBeth! She tried to run faster, but the muck kept sucking at her sneakers. The thing behind her was getting closer. ElsBeth's heart raced! She couldn't go any faster and it was almost upon her. . . .

ElsBeth collapsed and waited for the end. But nothing happened. And instead of slimy mud, ElsBeth felt warm and friendly hands on her forehead. And her grandmother's musical voice was saying, "Wake up, dear. It's time to get up."

ElsBeth blinked. It was morning. The sun was already up and she was tangled up wrong way to in the half-moon comforter on her little captain's bed. Sylvanas was perched on the headboard looking both aloof and concerned at the same time. And there was her grandmother, smiling slightly. She still looked distracted, but the important thing was that she was there.

ElsBeth relaxed. It was just a bad dream. But Grandmother had already cautioned her that a witch's dreams can be important. She must write everything down in her diary before she forgot.

ElsBeth grabbed the small leather-bound book she always kept on her bedside table. She pulled the lavender velvet ribbon, opening the diary to the next blank page. The silver bat weighting the end of the ribbon flashed in the morning sun, sending its reflection so it looked like a small bat was flitting about the room. The little witch began scribbling everything she could remember.

This was the first dream she'd had since Halloween. Then she had dreamt of the pirate Billy Bowlegs and his awesome treasure. And that dream turned out to be true!

While ElsBeth wrote away, Hannah backed into the rocking chair by the bed. The older witch shook her head and said to herself, "This isn't good. This is just *not* good." Hannah seemed to be in some kind of trance. She patted ElsBeth's head and slowly stood up, then wandered out, seeming to forget that ElsBeth was even there.

ElsBeth had never felt so alone as she watched her grandmother leave without even inquiring about her dream.

"What could be wrong with Grandmother?" she wondered again as she got herself dressed and ready for school.

Magical Moon

Chapter IV
SCHOOL – AGAIN!

When ElsBeth arrived at the schoolyard that day, she felt full of confidence. She definitely knew what a quotient was now, and she knew several practical reasons why anyone would even want to know about such a thing! Mathematics had become a very useful tool, in her opinion.

She was finally ready for Ms. Finch.

"Just go ahead and ask me for a quotient," ElsBeth frowned and muttered to herself as she passed through the large oaken doors of the Elementary School.

Hillman-Jones bumped into her, accidentally on purpose, and said quietly under his breath so there were no witnesses, "You'll never pass second grade, ElsBeth. Too bad you're so dumb."

ElsBeth lost her temper, an unfortunate failing of hers, and pushed him back. Just then Ms. Finch appeared outside the classroom door. Was the teacher psychic?

"I saw that, Ms. Thistle! Apparently no one has taught you the proper behavior for a young lady. Perhaps we need to make your detention permanent. No . . ."

The teacher's diabolical mind was working overtime. ElsBeth could almost see the dark thoughts flash by in Ms. Finch's head.

"Maybe you should stay back and study decorum while everyone else goes on the field trip to Boston next week. Yes. That will teach you a lesson."

At that point the school principal, Dr. Titcomb, popped his silver head out of his office and frowned at Ms. Finch. "Elvira, could I see you in my office for a moment?" It came out as more of an order than a question. Ms. Finch looked a little afraid and resentful at the same time. She sent a withering glance at ElsBeth and headed down the hall.

Five minutes later Ms. Finch came back to the classroom looking flushed, and ElsBeth was relieved that nothing more was said about her not going to Boston.

Spelling and reading flew by that morning. Today math came right after lunch and ElsBeth was actually looking forward to it for a change. She was completely ready, thanks to Badinoff's superb instruction.

Ms. Finch put the question up on the board, squealing the chalk for as long as possible. The students covered their ears and grimaced in pain.

The question she asked today was . . . "100 divided by 5 = ?"

Wow, Professor Badinoff had even anticipated Ms. Finch's exact question!

ElsBeth was so excited. She instantly raised her hand straight up. She would prove to Ms. Finch and that rotten Robert Hillman-Jones she was not dumb.

Ms. Finch, however, turned a blind eye to ElsBeth. It was as if the young witch didn't exist. ElsBeth quickly looked down at her body to ensure she hadn't gone invisible (a thing that can sometimes happen with witches). But ElsBeth was still there.

Ms. Finch glared down each row. No one else had raised a hand. Finally the teacher spotted a victim. Her eyes stopped at Nelson Hamm. Nelson's ears were bright red again and sticking out particularly far today, due to an unfortunate haircut at Barber Bernie's Hair Emporium last Saturday.

Nelson had been staring at Amy's blond curls, and was far-away in thought. He was imagining saving little Amy from a ferocious, fire-breathing dragon. He was right at the critical moment when Ms. Finch's icy voice cut through.

"Mr. Hamm, what is the quotient to this problem?" She tapped the blackboard loudly to emphasize the question.

Nelson also had no idea what a quotient was and sputtered several times before finally guessing. "Twenty?" he said timidly.

He had the answer right so Ms. Finch could only criticize his hesitancy. "Well, are you quite sure about that?" she snapped back.

Nelson sputtered some more.

Ms. Finch turned her stony face toward Robert Hillman-Jones and softened a bit. Robert was her favorite. "Robert, I'm sure you know the answer to this problem and won't have to equivocate."

Robert Hillman-Jones wasn't sure that twenty was the answer, either. And he definitely wasn't sure what "equivocate" meant. But he figured it had something to do with sounding uncertain. So he took a chance and replied in a voice full of confidence. (What the heck, he thought, the weirdo teacher liked him anyway and he might score some more points with her if he were right.) "Ms. Finch, the answer to this problem is clearly twenty!"

Ms. Finch let out a rare smile in Robert's direction, "Yes, Robert." Then she glared at the rest of the class and added, "At least *one* student in this class has been paying attention."

ElsBeth was ready to blow a gasket. For most of the day Hillman-Jones had been shooting dried wasabi peas through a straw at the girls. The last thing he had been doing was paying attention. ElsBeth was not going to stand by silently while he got away with this. It was wrong! She started to turn red and huff.

Ms. Finch raised an over-plucked eyebrow in ElsBeth's direction.

Fortunately, however, at that moment, Sylvanas the cat, in all his feline majesty, plopped his fluffy black self on the windowsill, distracting ElsBeth from doing something she was sure to regret.

The imposing cat let out a distinct hiss in Ms. Finch's direction.

The teacher looked over at the window and immediately jumped back behind her desk, stark terror stamped on her pinched face.

The magical cat seemed quite satisfied with that reaction. Ms. Finch would not dare to mess with ElsBeth, no matter the reason, when Sylvanas was there to intervene.

His action on ElsBeth's behalf complete, and having several other bits of mischief scheduled to be stirred up elsewhere just then, the magnificent cat disappeared from the windowsill, quicker than the eye could follow. Only the little witch and the teacher had observed his mysterious and brief appearance.

And ElsBeth had cooled off. Boy, that was a close one. Disaster had been narrowly avoided. She owed Sylvanas. Again.

Bartholomew Before He Was a Frog

Chapter V
TROUBLE BETWEEN THE WITCHES

That evening after another detention (during which even she would have to admit that her penmanship *had* improved nicely), ElsBeth again wound up in the garden with Bartholomew.

The huge frog was leaning back against the maple tree. He seemed deep in thought as ElsBeth sat on his green garden stool and looked at her friend. Before she said anything the frog croaked sympathetically, "I know, Ms. Finch isn't fair."

ElsBeth was taken by surprise. "How did you know what happened, Bartholomew?"

"Sylvanas," Bartholomew replied. No further explanation was needed.

ElsBeth, and everyone else with the slightest magical perception for miles around, was quite aware that Sylvanas was a compulsive gossip and meddler. Of course he would have passed on this juicy tidbit.

"Yes, well, she isn't fair. What can I do, Bartholomew? I want to go to Boston. I've never been off Cape and *everyone* is going." ElsBeth was actually whining a little. Quite unbecoming in a witch.

Bartholomew was understanding, though. "Don't worry, little one. Ms. Finch won't actually keep you here. She just enjoys making students feel upset. Unfortunately some people are like that.

"But I need to warn you," the frog continued ominously. "Not everywhere is like Cape Cod. There are things you will see in Boston that might scare you. It is an old place – lots of magic there."

What was happening here? Bartholomew had never before cautioned her about anything. He was an extremely brave frog and she knew he frowned upon cowardice above all else.

"What do you mean, Bartholomew? What should I be afraid of?"

Bartholomew just shook his head. "Nothing, little one, really. You should never walk in fear. But it is a wise individual who pays attention when the storm clouds gather and the enemy grows strong," he added wisely.

ElsBeth wrinkled her forehead, completely confused.

"Just pay attention and you'll be fine," the frog summarized in a tone that said "that was that".

ElsBeth wondered what she was supposed to pay attention to. She looked at Bartholomew in the fading light. The frog sat very still, and for just a moment ElsBeth saw him as the handsome Indian prince he had once been. His now deep brown eyes held many secrets. ElsBeth blinked twice, and once more only a simple, though exceptionally large, green frog leaned against the tree. ElsBeth felt better somehow after their little talk. She smiled at Bartholomew and headed off for supper.

As she skipped up the path toward the house, dark clouds swept in fast and low from the ocean. The pink and lavender Victorian house with its lacy curlicues was backlit by the towering storm clouds, and lightning played to and fro. ElsBeth watched in amazement. Weather was unpredictable on the Cape, but she had never before seen a storm move in this fast.

A large drop of rain plopped on her nose and in a split second she was drenched. She scooted up the steps onto the wide pine planks of the front porch and looked back. Outlined by the lightning against the clouds was the faint form of a face. It reminded her of someone, but she couldn't think who it was. She stood there soaked to the skin puzzling over the apparition. Then the wonderful smells of Grandmother's cranberry-orange bread pudding penetrated her consciousness.

"Grandmother, you made my other favorite!"

ElsBeth's grandmother was holding the bowl of golden pudding with bits of red and orange fruit sticking out on top, and suddenly all else was forgotten.

"Yes, ElsBeth, I thought we should have a special dinner. And after that we need to talk."

ElsBeth was too interested in pudding to notice the gravity in her grandmother's words.

After dinner ElsBeth completed her homework and her chores (even witches have to do chores every day). Then she and Grandmother curled up in the living room. A small fire crackled orange and red, sending a welcoming scent of cedar into the room. The evenings were still cool, and a fire took the chill off. The two witches settled in the comfortable wing chairs by the fireplace and sipped their cocoa, ElsBeth's steaming from her favorite bat mug and Hannah's in the big green cup that looked a little like Bartholomew.

"ElsBeth, you come from a long line of respected witches. We've talked about this before, but as a witch you have certain duties. You know we are responsible to see that the animals and plants and villagers are looked after, that the weather is kept somewhat under control, and that the magical creatures in our area are safeguarded. Those are our most important duties."

"Yes, Grandmother," ElsBeth replied earnestly.

"Well, ElsBeth, I know you are hoping to go to Boston. This is difficult for me to explain, but there hasn't been a competent witch in Boston for over two hundred years. There are all kinds of troubled ghosts, ghouls, goblins and restless spirits there, though. The city is really out of control – magically speaking.

"No one knows why, but witches can't seem to stand more than a day in the city before they just go mad. In fact, that's why all the witches moved back to Salem. It's a mystery no one's been able to penetrate, and believe me, many of us have tried over the years!" she added with a lot of feeling.

"Now, I know you have your heart set on going with the class on this field trip. And I know you'd only be in the city proper for several hours, but I'm quite concerned. What with the fairy situation and . . . well, the recent storms here on the Cape and everything else, I have my hands full right now. I just don't think I can be worrying about you in Boston, too."

ElsBeth was crushed. Did this mean her grandmother would not sign the permission slip?

Then suddenly her grandmother stopped speaking and looked a little muddled.

And happily for ElsBeth, no more was said about the subject that night.

But later in her little captain's bed, snug in her pink bat pajamas, ElsBeth, for the first time in her life, was upset with her grandmother. "How could she even imagine not letting me go on this trip?" ElsBeth began thinking up arguments she could use to change her elder's mind. ElsBeth had to get her grandmother to stop worrying. She could handle the trip. She just knew it!

ElsBeth glanced out the window at the clouds passing in front of the moon. She saw her familiar, Professor Badinoff, fly by, his large wings creating an inky shadow that chased over the ground. She wanted to discuss this difficult situation with the helpful bat.

"Professor!" she called out. But he was too far away to hear.

ElsBeth's mind went round and round on the sticky problem.

"What should I do?" she whispered again and again, as she fell into a restless slumber.

ElsBeth's Friends
Mehetabel and Thelonius Chipmunk

Chapter VI
SYLVANAS "HELPS OUT"

"I'm wearing my lime green Capri pants with the purple hoodie, and I've got this great new backpack with tons of pockets, *and* my mother is letting me wear the latest sea-glass necklace she created for her new jewelry line!" Veronica told the admiring girls crowded around her.

Veronica was always figuring out what to wear. Well, ElsBeth didn't really want to hear about Veronica's outfit for the Boston field trip when she wasn't even sure she'd be allowed to go. Her mind drifted, imagining everyone going – Robert Hillman-Jones, Johnny Twofeathers, Nelson, Amy – all the kids, even the Nye twins, who were being home schooled, were going to go.

Out of the corner of her eye, ElsBeth thought she saw a face disappear behind the apple tree. She started toward the corner of the playground to investigate. She could hear a rustling noise from behind the tree as she approached. And the air smelled funny, just like it does after a late summer thunderstorm. As she got even closer, she felt cold and a little afraid. Then, just before she reached the tree . . . the bell rang. The second graders began running. No one ever took a chance on being late to Ms. Finch's roll call – ever. ElsBeth had to go, but who . . . or what was behind the tree?

The last class period that day was history, one of ElsBeth's favorite subjects. And today they were learning about Indian tribes in New England. There were the

Algonquins, the Iroquois, the Nipmucs, the Abenakis and the Wampanoags, to name a few. Johnny Twofeathers was essentially Wampanoag royalty, though you'd never know it. He wasn't stuck up or anything. In fact, he seemed embarrassed today. Perhaps it was because Ms. Finch kept calling the Native Americans "savages". And each time she said the word she glanced over at Johnny, as if she expected him to protest. ElsBeth thought Ms. Finch was trying to get Johnny to lose his temper.

What Ms. Finch didn't appreciate was that Johnny never lost his temper. He was the least likely kid to ever get detention. It wasn't that he was a goody-two-shoes like Robert Hillman-Jones tried to be sometimes. Johnny was just a truly good person. ElsBeth counted herself lucky to have such a friend. She started thinking about all the wonderful Indians she knew . . . and then found herself daydreaming again.

Ms. Finch sharply interrupted ElsBeth's thoughts on the Indian nations by rapping hard on the blackboard with her wooden pointer. It appears that many of the young students had wandered off while the teacher went on and on about the least interesting aspects of Indian culture (a hard thing to do, since Indian culture is actually completely fascinating). Luckily ElsBeth wasn't singled out for daydreaming, this time.

In fact, it turned out that Ms. Finch was on an entirely different subject than Indian history now.

"I need all of your permission slips for the trip to Boston. Please hand them forward."

"Oh no!" ElsBeth said to herself, she had *totally* forgotten they were due today. She hadn't even had another chance to talk to Grandmother about signing hers.

ElsBeth looked around guiltily. Everyone seemed to be pulling a note from his or her lunch box or backpack. That is, everyone except Robert Hillman-Jones. Was it possible his parents didn't want him to go, either?

Hillman-Jones raised his hand, smiling brightly at Ms. Finch. Ms. Finch's face seemed to crack slightly as a small smile broke through her frown lines. "Yes, Robert?"

"My father is in New York this week and my mother is in L.A, so I don't have a note. My father said he would call the principal this evening and authorize my going."

Ms. Finch's face almost cracked again. Robert was, hands down, her favorite, but the crabby teacher hated any, that is *any*, deviation from the rules.

"Permission slips are *required,* Robert." And she turned her back on the surprised student and faced the blackboard.

Hillman-Jones had rarely been refused anything in his short, expensive life. For once he was speechless.

"Now children, pass in the slips!" Ms. Finch also hated repeating herself.

They hurried to follow her directions before some sort of eruption took place.

Nelson Hamm nervously dropped his slip several times. Ms. Finch always got to Nelson. His ears were practically neon right now. He finally got it together and passed it forward.

Veronica whispered, "ElsBeth, where is your note?"

Before ElsBeth had time to answer, the large black cat appeared on the windowsill again, and grinned at ElsBeth. ElsBeth began to hope.

And just as suddenly, the brisk North Wind burst in and swept through the classroom, creating miniature whirlpools as he swirled through. The North Wind particularly enjoyed whipping up Ms. Finch's hair to a spiky peak on top of her head and blowing her glasses off.

Permission slips went every which way! Many flew out the window and over the playground.

Ms. Finch's hair continued to stand on end. Whether that was because she spotted Sylvanas staring at her, or because the wind kept whipping about her head, wasn't clear.

"ElsBeth!" the teacher shouted. "Get that cat out of here!"

Just then Sylvanas leapt several feet in the air, sailing in a most graceful fashion for such an oversized cat, and landed neatly in the center of Ms. Finch's large oak desk. He arched his back slowly and hissed up at the Finch. He then casually turned around, and sailed back through the window. The North Wind followed, with more permission slips trialing after, as he, too, dramatically swept away.

The children were stunned. Ms. Finch, usually *extremely* well organized and in control, was at a loss. The trip was tomorrow. She would have no time to get new slips printed and sent home. At least three days notice was required. How would she explain this to the principal? In the heat of the moment, under pressure, she made a snap decision.

"Right. Very well. It looks like we'll all be going. Class dismissed!"

ElsBeth was in a daze. She could go on the trip! Deep down she knew it wasn't *completely* honest. But a little voice inside quickly piped up with excuses. . . . "Grandmother never *exactly* said I couldn't go. She was just concerned. If I'm very careful there will be nothing to worry about. I'm just a small witch, and I won't be in Boston more than twenty-four hours. I get along well with all magical creatures. Grandmother will never know, and I shouldn't bother her with this right now. Besides, Sylvanas wouldn't have helped me like this unless he thought I should go."

In short order ElsBeth had it completely and well justified why she should not tell her grandmother, though she couldn't help struggling with feeling it wasn't *quite* right.

Finally, she made up her mind. "I'm almost through second grade. I'm going to have to make my own decisions and take responsibility for my own life sooner or later. It might as well be now!" And with a determined look on her face (and only a few niggling guilt feelings still prickling at her conscience), the small witch headed out from school.

On her way home the handsome blue heron, Thaddeus Crane, flew low by the little witch. He called out, "ElsBeth, what's happening? Your grandmother is not herself, and you seem different and upset, too. All the marsh creatures are worried."

ElsBeth *did* have some things on her mind, but she didn't feel she could burden the kindly bird with all that.

"It's OK, Thaddeus. It's just the fairies again. Grandmother's had a lot to handle with them lately. That's all."

Thaddeus's piercing eyes seemed to look right through ElsBeth.

"I don't think that *is* all, ElsBeth," he said sternly. Then his voiced warmed again. "Remember, we marsh birds are here if you need us." He flapped slowly away and reminded ElsBeth, "We all love you and Hannah. Remember your friends."

Thaddeus swooped round in a lazy circle, tipped his wings in salute, and was off to the nearby salt marshes for dinner.

ElsBeth scuffed down the crushed shell drive not noticing all the animals who watched her pass. Othello, the thoughtful old owl, blinked his huge yellow eyes and followed ElsBeth's small figure with concern. "There is something wrong with that young witch," he hooted to himself.

Persephone, the beautiful yellow coyote, stepped along beside ElsBeth, well hidden in the woods. She made no sound as she padded through the bushes, while ElsBeth crunched noisily down the center of the drive. Persephone was a sensitive creature. She wasn't going to intrude on the little witch's thoughts, but she followed closely, protectively watching over ElsBeth the whole way home.

The fat gray squirrels stopped their endless play and chattered to each other as ElsBeth went by. And Thelonius Chipmunk, her wildly talented neighbor, paused in his musically expressive nut cracking to observe the witch's unusually quiet mood.

"That's odd," he said to Mehetabel, his mate. "ElsBeth always wants to hear my latest tunes when she goes by. I wonder what gives?"

Mehetabel was busy grooming her beautiful reddish fur and aligning her black stripes to best advantage. "You can never tell with witches. Strange and unpredictable creatures they are," she added, while vainly admiring herself in a pool of collected rainwater.

Thelonius thought, "You're a more vain and unpredictable creature than any witch I ever met." But he carefully kept his mouth shut. A harmonious marriage in the chipmunk world required a lot of restraint! And he went back to steadily gathering nuts and making new music. Thelonius operated on the guiding principle that one could never have too many nuts stored up for a Cape winter.

Sylvanas had been keeping an eye out for ElsBeth, too, waiting for her by the edge of the garden.

ElsBeth kept walking, not noticing the huge cat until she nearly stepped on his splendid tail.

"Oh, sorry Sylvanas," she said automatically.

She continued walking completely unaware that the magical cat was waiting to speak with her.

ElsBeth had been thinking she couldn't easily talk to Grandmother now, and lately Bartholomew wasn't much better. She might have to try taking things up with Sylvanas again. She wasn't happy about this, though. Sylvanas was exceptional in many ways, but not to talk to. The cat almost never gave a straight answer to any question put to him. Still, she needed to discuss things with *someone*, and decided it would have to be the mischievous Sylvanas after all.

The black cat had kept up with ElsBeth as she had unseeingly paced back and forth along the drive. ElsBeth finally turned and saw him. Sylvanas somehow managed to look down on ElsBeth, while actually looking up at the young witch. Sylvanas was tricky that way. Everyone always felt they were beneath Sylvanas somehow.

Persephone watched as the two magical beings spoke. The small witch looked agitated and the imposing cat looked . . . well . . . imposing. The coyote wondered what they were saying, but she had difficulty understanding English. She could see they were planning something. Coyotes were exceptionally good at picking up others' intentions. They had to be very aware to survive in the odd world of people. "What exactly are ElsBeth and Sylvanas up to?" she thought again. The beautiful creature decided she had better keep an eye on these two. Something was definitely going on.

Hannah seemed even more worried at dinner that evening. The whole wheat pineapple upside-down-cake was served right side up. Dessert was served before the main course and they had no honey milk. There was no happy chatter, practicing of incantations, crystal ball readings or anything interesting. Things at Six Druid Lane were definitely not normal. Even for a magical family.

Only Sylvanas was his usual self. It was as if the cat had a cunning plan he was keeping to himself. He licked at the heavy cream on his dessert and purred with a satisfied grin.

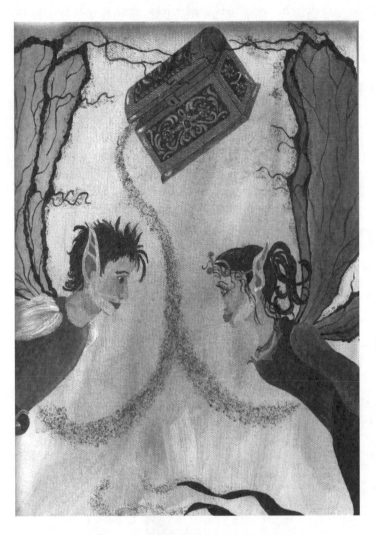

Troublesome Fairies

Chapter VII
BOSTON OR BUST

ElsBeth woke up from a curious dream on the day of the class trip. In the dream there was this face that looked so familiar. There was a tunnel, and rooms and rooms full of gold and jewels. What did it all mean?

Even though she got up late, she took a few minutes to write down everything from the dream in her diary. She marked her place with the velvet ribbon and rubbed the silver bat at the end for luck. She threw on the clothes at the front of her closet and ran down to breakfast.

She found Grandmother in the kitchen as usual. The older witch's fluffy gray hair and her face were decorated with flour dustings here and there. Hannah Goodspell looked pale and exhausted, but fresh-baked, hot cranberry scones were on the table, loaded with cream cheese, and just waiting for ElsBeth.

For once ElsBeth didn't want to take her time over breakfast, though, and chatter away to her grandmother. She quickly gulped down her yogurt with nuts and berries and grabbed a cranberry scone. She kissed her grandmother on the tip of her floury nose and gave her an extra big hug, while carefully not looking the older witch in the eye. She waved at the moon-faced grandfather clock in the corner, who winked back cheerily, and she was out the door.

When ElsBeth got to the school yard, she found most of her classmates dressed as if they were going to see the President of the United States!

Amy had on a pink satin creation from Laura Ashley with patent leather shoes that shined brilliantly in the sun.

Veronica looked like a little Paris Hilton, though with many more layers of clothes on.

Nelson Hamm sported a bow tie!

Carmen had on a yellow confirmation dress with pale orange tights. Carmen's mother was well known around town for minor color blindness. At least Carmen looked great in yellow, though the orange tights made her look a little like a bird.

Jimmy Miller was trying to stuff the yellow rain slicker his father had insisted he take into his backpack, but it wouldn't quite fit. Jimmy's family had been fishermen forever and his father was a firm believer in being prepared for any weather condition. This meant one always had a heavy yellow slicker and an extra-heavy-duty flashlight at hand. After all, it could be sunny on the Cape one minute and a full storm with gale winds could hit the next.

The studious Lisa Lee had on a lovely Chinese silk outfit. With her oversized glasses she looked like a midget Chinese grandmother, but she was also oddly elegant. She had an interesting brown belt holding her red padded jacket together.

Johnny Twofeathers showed up at the last minute in pressed khakis, a crisp white button-down shirt, striped tie and a navy blazer. He looked like a miniature, well-tanned, Harvard law student. He did, however, carry an oversized backpack with dozens of pockets that looked suspiciously practical.

ElsBeth looked down at her own clothes. She had on her oldest purple tights, a denim skirt and a lavender hooded sweater that was slightly too small. Wow, she felt embarrassed! She had left so quickly this morning that she hadn't even considered what to wear on the big day – their first class trip all the way to the city. The children would, in essence, be representing their entire school, all of Cape Cod, even. Boy, did she mess up!

But ElsBeth was soon distracted from these dark thoughts as Robert Hillman-Jones arrived in his uncle's classic, perfectly restored, Skylight Blue, 1964½ Mustang, just as the final bell rang.

Everyone was here, except the Nye twins. The girls had been completely ecstatic when they were told they were to be included in the school trip. They usually had to go everywhere with their mother – the major downside to the home school program in their opinion. But a case of the measles destined the fun-loving redheads to miss out on this great opportunity.

**Uncle Preston's
1964½ Skylight Blue Mustang**

Chapter VIII
ALL ABOARD THE MAGIC BUS

"Stop shoving!"

"You stop shoving!" Frankie's stocky frame was blocking the kids behind him from getting seated.

Frankie'd had to run back for his lunch box. He was pretty focused when it came to food, but in the excitement of the trip he'd gotten into a small disagreement with Nelson over which team was the best – the New England Patriots or the Boston Red Sox – and in the heated debate Frankie forgot his lunch.

Frankie saw that the boys had taken the back seats and the girls had started filling in from there. And Frankie was now stuck in the middle of the girls.

This was just not happening! Frankie was in the second grade – almost done with second grade – there was no way he was sitting with a girl.

At that moment Hillman-Jones shoved his way past several girls. "Frankie, we're sitting here." Hillman-Jones pushed Amy's slight frame out of the way and plunked down in the seat in front of Veronica. "We can definitely cause more trouble from the middle," he added with an evil grin, staring down Veronica at the same time.

Nelson immediately jumped up to defend Amy, who had been pushed back into the boy's section. But Ms. Finch's abrupt appearance at the front of the bus stopped Nelson cold.

Nelson was pretty scrawny, but when it came to Amy the skinny boy knew no fear – except Ms. Finch. He slowly disappeared back into his seat.

Ms. Finch, with her unfailing radar, had sensed the children's growing joy and promptly arrived to crush it. And with the teacher now present, the children quickly settled into their seats.

ElsBeth was next to Lisa Lee. Lisa's mysterious backpack, which was covered in strange symbols all around a bright red dragon, took up most of the seat. The backpack was like having another squat kid between the two girls, and ElsBeth was scrunched up against the window. And every once in a while the bag seemed to move on its own. ElsBeth was intrigued.

ElsBeth and many of the other kids had never been on a bus before. ElsBeth, in fact, had rarely been in a car. The Cape Cod witches didn't particularly find it necessary to go in motorized vehicles. And Grandmother was quite opposed to fossil fuels – she said they hurt the environment – so a bus ride was going to be quite an experience. ElsBeth only hoped the bus wouldn't use too much fossil fuel.

ElsBeth could see the bus driver outside the window. He was pretty famous among the school children. McTodd MacSweeney was a dashing young fellow from farther down Cape. McTodd was only five feet and one inch tall, which had earned him the nickname "Big Mac". The driver was most admired, though, for also being an expert Irish sword dancer and bagpiper. His performances on Saint Patty's day drew crowds from all across the Cape.

The athletic Big Mac jumped aboard, bowing neatly to the children, just as Ms. Finch began to call roll.

Each student answered up crisply when his or her name was called. Except Nelson, that is, who stuttered a bit when it was his turn – Ms. Finch just made him so nervous!

As the teacher wrapped up the list with Frankie Sylvester's name, a tall stranger swung gracefully up the steps of the yellow Bluebird bus.

The kids were surprised. This was a small town and everybody knew absolutely everybody. And no one had ever seen this man before. Ms. Finch sensed she had lost the children's undivided attention (something she especially demanded during roll calls – or else).

She turned around, and her breath caught in her throat. Before her was the most handsome man she had ever seen. Unconsciously she fluffed her short blue-black hair. Then remembering herself and her position, she immediately turned back to the no-nonsense activity of organizing the children.

When she finished, she again turned to the gorgeous man behind her. "May I help you?" she asked, pretending she was completely disinterested in the stunning stranger.

The tall man closed the short distance between them. He stood close to the teacher. Her cold heart beat faster.

His voice was rich and warm and vaguely foreign. "Are you Elvira Finch?"

"Yes," Ms. Finch purred as she looked into those midnight blue eyes framed by thick black lashes.

The children looked on, fascinated.

"Principal Titcomb asked me to assist you today in guiding the students through the Boston Freedom Trail and museums. Mrs. Bottomley is . . . ill," he added with no further explanation.

"I'm Xavier Saint Georges. Charmed to meet you, Elvira," he added with a slight and knowing smile.

"Yes," Ms. Finch purred again. The fearsome teacher seemed hypnotized.

Xavier placed his manicured hands on the teacher's thin shoulders and gently guided her to a seat at the front of the bus.

Ms. Finch smoothed her skirt, shook herself a little, and cooed, "We're all set, Mr. MacSweeney."

Just as Big Mac was shutting the door, a small black streak barreled through the opening.

Sylvanas made it past Ms. Finch easily. The teacher was still staring dreamily at Xavier.

None of the kids noticed as the black blur shot onto the back of a seat, then into a storage area overhead.

Even ElsBeth missed Sylvanas's entrance. Veronica was tapping her shoulder from across the aisle at that moment.

"Did you see that? Ms. Finch is in love, and I don't blame her." Veronica was more interested in boys than she should have been, in ElsBeth's opinion.

ElsBeth turned back toward the handsome man, and for some reason she couldn't identify felt an immediate uneasiness. There was something familiar about him, but there was something not quite right about him, too. She just couldn't put her finger on it.

Big Mac put the yellow bus in gear, and with hisses and puffs the second grade class – with two important additions – was off.

As they headed away from the salt marshes and cranberry bogs of home, the scrub pines and twisted oaks gave way. Soon the view opened up and on the right was a large thatch-roofed building. It looked like something out of a fairy tale. It was called the Christmas Tree Shop. How wonderful! ElsBeth liked that. She couldn't wait to tell her grandmother about it.

Then, as the big yellow bus rumbled across the Sagamore Bridge, and over the canal that separated the Cape from the mainland, ElsBeth suddenly felt a shift. The world looked a little different. The sun was less bright. The shadows darker. The air less sweet.

"That's odd," ElsBeth said to herself. A prolonged hiss sounded directly above her. "That's even odder," the witch observed.

Up in the front of the bus McTodd had changed his Nantucket fishing cap for a bright red Boston Red Sox baseball hat. They were off Cape now for sure.

As the bus rumbled along Pilgrim Highway, they were passed by intense, serious-looking commuters heading north, as well. ElsBeth noticed most were dressed in dark blue jackets and pink shirts with colorful ties. She thought this might be some kind of uniform.

The little witch found it all so interesting!

On the right she saw swans swimming up a small creek. At least that was just like on the Cape.

They soon passed Plymouth, and on the left there was a huge Indian totem pole in front of a rest area just off the highway. The feather headdress on top of the pole looked majestic as it towered above the roofline of MacDonald's. ElsBeth hadn't known that Indians had invented MacDonald's!

Then, for just a moment, ElsBeth saw a flickering image – a grim-faced pilgrim in a tall black hat, beside a pale woman in a long homespun dress, holding the hand of a small child with haunted eyes. And standing tall, right next to them, was a muscular Indian, looking sad. There was something disturbing about them.

But the bus sped on down the highway. And when ElsBeth looked back, there was only the totem pole. "Strange again," she mumbled to herself.

Lisa, her seatmate, wasn't very talkative – ever. So ElsBeth had plenty of time to think. She turned her attention to Grandmother. ElsBeth knew well that fairies could cause enormous concern. Getting into mischief was their favorite thing to do, particularly when they were angry about something. And even more particularly with royal fairies.

The fairies had helped ElsBeth and Johnny Twofeathers escape from the pirate cave last Halloween. But at the same time they'd been naughty and annoying. They *loved* being contrary. They'd been locked in a velvet-lined chest a couple of centuries ago, and they'd had plenty of time to sleep and dream – especially to dream of ways to cause all kinds of chaos!

But was it just the fairies causing all the recent problems in the village? There'd been the fistfight that broke out at the town meeting over someone's shockingly improper grammar. Then there was all the strange weather, and the manatee found lost at a nearby town dock.

And what about the whales bumping into the fishing boats, and the seagulls dropping shells on the steps of the Town Hall, and the balloon festival where all the balloons blew out to sea and had to be rescued by the Coast Guard? Not to mention what happened to old lady Cahoon's wig!

It did seem that a lot of inexplicable things were going on in the village lately.

Lisa's quiet but precisely spoken words broke in on ElsBeth's thoughts. "Magical beings can cause trouble."

ElsBeth did a double take at her mysterious classmate. "Excuse me, Lisa. What did you just say?"

"It is a well known fact that supernatural beings are behind a large percentage of seemingly inexplicable happenings," the little Oriental girl explained.

ElsBeth had never heard this many words spoken aloud in a row by Lisa before. "What do you mean?" ElsBeth finally asked.

"Well, clearly you were disturbed by the ghosts in Plymouth, leading logically to thoughts about the recent strange happenings in town, and ending precisely in your concern about Miss Cahoon's wig situation."

"Wow, Lisa, how . . . how did you know all that?!"

"Elementary, I saw them, too."

"Well . . . how did you know I was thinking about Miss Cahoon's wig?!"

"You were patting your hair. An obvious conclusion, really."

ElsBeth was speechless. But just then she noticed a small hill on the right topped by a sign that said "Pleasant Mountain Pet Rest". The two girls glanced out the window and saw a beautiful Dalmatian being chased by a yipping black and white Chihuahua. Several orange and black cats looked on with disapproval, while a sad Labrador retriever puppy sat on his hind legs as if begging to be hugged.

ElsBeth and Lisa looked quickly at each other, and then back at the cemetery, which was now completely empty.

Lisa nodded slowly, "This is going to be an interesting trip." She folded her hands neatly in her lap and was perfectly still again.

Every few miles as the bus rumbled along, ElsBeth noticed figures that seemed out of place. In Marshfield there were several Indians in yellow buckskins chasing a white wolf. There was a man dressed as an old-fashioned locomotive engineer hovering over the train tracks just south of Braintree.

As they approached the city, a horse and rider passed by. The rider carried a lantern and leaned low, urging his horse to go faster. He seemed to be waving at ElsBeth. ElsBeth thought he looked like the picture of Paul Revere that Ms. Finch had put up in the classroom when they studied the American Revolution.

Lisa made no further comment. She just looked quietly intelligent, as usual.

The other children chattered excitedly. There was no serious monkey business, of course. Ms. Finch would have been on them in a New York second (whatever that was) if anyone was significantly misbehaving.

Sitting up front and talking in hushed tones with the striking Xavier, Ms. Finch was thoroughly distracted – sufficiently so that the children's spirits were able to rise, along with the sound level, to that of a normal busload of second graders.

And finally they reached the edge of the city. Boston! Home of the Boston Tea Party – Revolutionaries – Freedom Fighters – the lot! Here it was with its beautiful tall buildings poking up into the sky – the John Hancock, the Prudential, Government Center. . . .

Lisa sat up interestedly when they passed the exit for Chinatown. You could see the bright blue tiled roofs of some of the buildings. But she quickly settled back as they flew on to the day's destination – the Boston Commons.

All this time, Sylvanas had indulged in one of his favorite activities – extreme napping. He had found Veronica's quilted knapsack and several emergency blankets and created a highly satisfactory bed for himself. He preferred an extra soft down comforter piled high with several Egyptian cotton pillows, of course, but he was able to rough it in a pinch. He quite happily slept through the seventy-five-odd miles from the Cape to the city.

He now stretched lazily and his big green eyes began to survey the local scenery. He hadn't been off Cape himself for close to two centuries. Things had certainly changed from the swampy cow paths and smelly marshes of the old settlement.

Sylvanas wasn't much interested in the amazing architecture of one of the first U.S. cities, though. That subject was really quite beneath him. But ghosts – that was another thing. Boston was full, stuffed, loaded and positively jam-packed with ghosts!

And somewhere in this gold mine of haunted spirits was the one with the answer to Hannah Goodspell's recent strange behavior. Sylvanas was sure of it! And this particular fat black cat fully intended to get some answers, even if it meant getting ElsBeth into a little hot water.

After all, he would just get her right back out of it again if it came to that.

With a long final stretch the cat was ready for action.

As the bus parked at the Commons near the swan boats, Ms. Finch reluctantly tore herself away from Xavier and began shouting instructions to her happy students. "Single file children. Off the bus. Line up *neatly* in groups of no more than three. *No* talking, Veronica!"

The children grabbed backpacks and jackets and headed down the aisle. Ms. Finch glared at each child, dampening spirits only slightly, however, as they moved to the front and hopped down off the bus.

Chapter IX
BUSTLING BUS LOADS

The children lined up with minimum fighting over who was in each group. Veronica and ElsBeth were together. Amy, Carmen and Lisa stood beside them. Robert Hillman-Jones formed the toughest pair with Frankie Sylvester. Johnny Twofeathers led his group with Nelson Hamm and Jimmy Miller.

Just then two other buses drove up and parked nearby, as the ever-vigilant Ms. Finch again called roll. The teacher marked off each child's name with a precise, black tick in her precisely-lined, neat, black notebook.

The Cape children looked on as two dozen students in cookie-cutter uniforms smartly stepped off the sparkling red bus parked next to MacSweeney's yellow pride and joy. The Cape children looked with considerably more interest as an old bus labeled "South Boston Elementary" puffed and wheezed into position next, and a hardy looking bunch of second graders tumbled and shoved their way off that beat up rust bucket.

The students from the uniformed group managed to look disinterested in the Cape Cod youngsters, but some of the South Boston kids spotted Frankie Sylvester and immediately began calling out rude questions like, "Hey, fat boy, you been eating too much cannoli or what?"

Ms. Finch quickly took control before Frankie could even get his fists up, "Frankie, eyes front!" Then, "Children, follow me!" She broke concentration long enough to look up dreamily at Xavier and added, "Mr.

Saint Georges . . ." in a soft, unFinchlike voice, inviting him to walk beside her.

Veronica turned back to ElsBeth, fingering her designer hoodie and flipped her hair. She pointed at the uniformed students and dared to whisper, "What snobs." She said this while scowling at a particularly pretty girl in a crisp, plaid, pleated skirt with matching Navy jacket and gleaming white socks that peeked above her tasseled loafers.

"Really, who do they think they are?" Veronica stuck out her tongue, a rare moment of childish behavior for her. Veronica prided herself on her maturity.

ElsBeth acknowledged Veronica without much attention. She didn't really understand what the big deal was with fancy clothes. ElsBeth didn't want to look a mess. She just liked to be comfortable working in the garden and hiking around the local trails. Though she did appreciate a good pair of boots and her L.L. Bean rain slicker – the wind and rain could really get through to you on the Cape without them.

At the head of the uniformed students stood a tall, sophisticated, middle-aged man. He was dressed a lot like Johnny Twofeathers, only many sizes larger. His candy-red framed reading glasses hung on a beaked nose.

Lisa, suddenly talkative again – at least for her – said, "Brahmin . . . Boston Brahmin."

ElsBeth said, "What?" surprised to hear Lisa speak up once more. The normally science-crazed girl was suddenly turning positively social.

"Boston Brahmin. Old money. Old family. They have to go into banking, law or politics. Teaching is the last choice – barely acceptable. Probably the black sheep of an old New England family," she added with a short nod.

ElsBeth, Veronica, Carmen and Amy stared with mouths wide open at their little classmate.

ElsBeth wasn't sure what Lisa was talking about, but didn't expect to get much more of an explanation, so she turned around to take in the surroundings.

Everything was lovely! The cherry and magnolia trees were in blossom, and the air was perfumed with sweet spring flowers, mixed with the tang of salt from the sea – though a trace of pollution did spoil the effect some.

There were a few fluffy white clouds in a bright blue sky. And the colors in the gardens were brilliant.

ElsBeth heaved a sigh. "We're in Boston. It's really not a bad place," she said to herself. Then suddenly a chill ran down her spine, in contradiction, perhaps, to her unfounded optimism.

Meanwhile, Sylvanas took his time getting off the bus. He waited until McTodd MacSweeney, the scrappy and now hungry bus driver, had stepped off and wandered toward a nearby doughnut stand.

Big Mac loved doughnuts. He had actually made a point of trying every single doughnut outlet from Provincetown to Hyannis. He was partial to Dunkin', but always hoped for even tastier treats, and searched these out with care. He was willing to experiment. MacSweeney considered himself an adventurous sort. And those double-glazed, chocolate mousse filled jellies he spotted in the distance looked like a bold taste treat. His step quickened as he approached the sweet-smelling stand.

Sylvanas was also passionate about doughnuts, no doubt at least one cause of his slight weight problem. But the cat was on a mission. There would be no doughnuts for now . . . er . . . perhaps that was too hasty, maybe a little later, he decided upon getting another whiff.

He leapt from the bus and in one quick bound was comfortably settled in a nearby elm tree, surveying the scene. "Yes," he purred to himself as he observed a city full of magic. "Boston was just the place for some answers."

Sylvanas Surveys the Swans of Boston Commons

Chapter X
THE GHOSTLY FREEDOM TRAIL

One of the park guides had on a cool brown outfit. He looked like Ben Franklin, except he was black. This caused a small debate, as most of the kids were pretty sure Ben Franklin was white. In any case, the Ben Franklin look-alike led the fascinated Cape group.

Following close behind were the matching outfits of what Lisa Lee had guessed were kids from a private school, headed up by the gentleman in the candy-red glasses, whom they now thought of as the "Boston Brahmin" as Lisa had called him.

Happily pushing and scuffling their way forward, the school children from South Boston brought up the rear of this expedition into the city's natural (and sometimes unnatural) history.

The students from the three groups were herded, more or less successfully, by their teachers behind the tour guide, "Ben Franklin", who had now been joined by a plump woman in a puffy cap and a wide brown skirt.

Ben Franklin and the plump lady began to tease a third guide who also arrived on the scene. He wore a red coat and had long white hair in a braided pigtail. On top of his head was what looked like a funny looking baseball cap.

"Red Coat" gathered the children closer and began to explain the British version of the history of Boston. Boston was a colony founded in the 1600's. ElsBeth was fascinated at this news because her grandmother came from the Old World in the 1600's! How interesting!

Apparently Boston Commons, where they now stood, used to be a swamp. And over there, where the gold-roofed State House overlooked the park, were once three hills – now gone to fill in the wetlands. There had even been streams where there was now just land.

Johnny Twofeathers was particularly interested in this. Even in his short life he had seen this happen. A wild wood was bulldozed flat and before you knew it there was a boring house with a perfectly green lawn, and perfect flowers – in the middle of some unnatural-colored bark. It just didn't seem right to the young Wampanoag.

He understood from his grandfather that when you took away a wood you could lose plants that were used for healing. And once all these places were "developed", the plants could no longer be found. His grandfather said the Native American people knew about more than two thousand plants that were used as medicine, and most of them were now gone. Johnny remembered seeing a plaque about this at the Heritage Plantation in the Town of Sandwich, too.

Johnny was disturbed by all this and vowed he would try to protect the environment in his town. ElsBeth gave Johnny a glance. She knew just what her friend was thinking, and she felt the same way.

The Red Coat guide had begun to move on and the children followed, taking in the sights and history with interest.

As they moved out of the park, ElsBeth was amazed by all the tall buildings, so close together. And the people moved so fast. Where were they going so quickly? And they didn't seem interested in any of the wonderful things around them. This was all strange to the young witch.

Veronica, Amy and Lisa were taking the city in stride. They had been to Boston before, as had Robert Hillman-Jones. But many of the rest of their group had never been off Cape. And they seemed ill at ease with the unaccustomed sights and sounds and smells.

ElsBeth looked at their confused faces and began to wonder if this trip had been such a great idea after all.

But the children moved raggedly along, trying to listen to Red Coat as he described battles, politics and the city's unique architecture. The interest of the children only began to lessen when they could no longer hear him above the noises of the city.

And the further they went, the more upset Veronica became. She was really irritated. Not about the history lesson. What got to Veronica was that she hated to be out-dressed, and there was no getting around it, the kids from the private school were sharp dressers. They had somehow managed some great individual looks while still wearing a school uniform. There were some absolutely beautiful hair pieces, rings and jewelry amongst the well-dressed little girls.

One girl had a stylish silver dragon pin with diamond eyes that decorated her beret, and another had a really cool, enameled, green-on-green frog with large yellow opal eyes.

When Veronica saw these she was really angry. "What's so great about semiprecious stones and diamonds anyway? My mother says they are 'blood diamonds'!" she added. "Kids get blown up in Africa trying to find the foolish things. That can't be cool!" She stamped her foot to make the point clear.

Next to the volcano that was Veronica walked Amy, the opposite in temperament. Making Veronica feel even worse, a handsome, dark-eyed, private school boy with a turban kept glancing shyly at Amy. And to Nelson Hamm's horror, Amy was glancing back!

Veronica noticed this and gave Amy a sharp little kick. "Stop it! You're encouraging him," Veronica hissed.

Amy looked down, embarrassed. And the turbaned boy quickly sped up to the rest of his group, which had moved closer to the Red Coat park ranger. Boys, particularly strange ones, always seemed to fall all over themselves when Amy was present.

Veronica had complained to ElsBeth about this before. "Amy never wears any color except pink. Her clothes are old-fashioned and she never cuts her hair. She has no sense of style," Veronica would sniff. "What is it about that little mouse, anyway?"

Veronica actually liked Amy a lot. And Amy was one of her best friends, after all. But Veronica was clearly a little jealous of her fashion-unconscious friend's ability to attract lots of attention from the boys.

As the drama unfolded up front, Carmen had fallen behind and the Southie girls began teasing, calling her "Big Bird" due to her yellow and orange outfit.

ElsBeth began to think it was better to be dressed in her old clothes. At least people didn't pick on you!

She had just come to this comforting conclusion when Robert Hillman-Jones bumped into her, accidentally on purpose as usual, and said, "Gee, ElsBeth, what's the matter? Your grandmother can't afford to buy you clothes that fit?"

ElsBeth was about to lose her temper when Ms. Finch tore her eyes from Xavier long enough to notice that the group had become disordered from her initially perfect formation. Ms. Finch would certainly have made a great Marine sergeant.

"Children, line-up! RIGHT NOW! Er . . . please," she added sweetly, smiling up at Xavier.

The children lined up. Nelson, who was now staring angrily at the back of the turbaned boy, almost got trampled in the process.

"We are about to enter one of the oldest cemeteries in the United States. It's called the Granary Cemetery. Many famous historical figures are buried here. Listen carefully to the ranger. He will give you all the details. Pay attention and write notes. You *will* be quizzed," the uncompromising teacher added with an underlying tone of threat.

Then she saw Xavier staring at her. She did her best to smile at the students and murmured, "It's for their own good. We have standards to maintain after all." On Ms. Finch the smile looked more like an expression caused by extreme stomach pains, and was *pretty* scary, but the children felt encouraged.

They quickly took out their notebooks, though. No telling how long Ms. Finch's good mood would last.

Red Coat started telling the three groups of students about the famous people buried in the graveyard. But ElsBeth was noticing the details of the ranger's costume. His coat was brick-red wool with lots of brass buttons and fancy gold braid on the shoulders. His white pants had six brass snaps at the bottom that went over his boots. He had on a vest, and his red coat had navy blue cuffs and lapels. ElsBeth thought it was quite interesting that a man dressed just like the ranger had appeared behind one of the gravestones. He seemed to be making fun of the ranger, and trying to get ElsBeth's attention.

Suddenly ElsBeth saw strangely dressed figures popping up beside gravestones everywhere. And they were all speaking to her at once!

On her right, next to his gravestone, was the famous Samuel Adams. He wore a fancy gray wig and called to ElsBeth, "Young witch, young witch, come here! I have some complaints that need to be addressed. This taxation without representation situation cannot be tolerated! No taxation without representation, I say!"

ElsBeth stared wide-eyed. She wasn't too sure what taxes were, but according to Mr. Adams they were definitely a bad thing. Especially if one weren't represented when one had them.

The ghosts of the real Ben Franklin's mother and father were arguing about their son. "What will he come up with next? We never should have sent him to the Latin School," shouted Ben's father. "That boy never could control his imagination after learning the classics. Next thing you know he'll try to harness lightning itself!" The chubby old fellow laughed at his own joke and then asked ElsBeth her opinion. "What do you think, young witch?"

ElsBeth had no thought in her head about that at all. Then Paul Revere jumped up on his horse and looked over the children shouting, "There's a witch nearby! Where is she? Let me through. We need to speak."

And other ghosts began clamoring at full shout! ElsBeth put her hands over her ears to shut them out.

Veronica said, "What's up, ElsBeth? It's not *that* noisy." It seemed ElsBeth was the only one who could see and hear them.

She tried to block out the ghosts, and found that if she concentrated on the tour guides and the real live people around her that the spirits began to fade.

Now the children were being led away from the cemetery, and ElsBeth could begin to relax. But she felt someone staring at her as she moved down the street. She turned around quickly and saw Xavier Saint Georges looking right at her with a twinkle in his eye. ElsBeth wasn't sure why, but the man didn't seem quite normal. ElsBeth began to wonder if he were a witch, too. But if he were a witch, then how could he stand Boston? She remembered that her grandmother had been quite specific that witches went mad in Boston.

Then the children from Boston's South End swarmed ahead and cut off her view of Xavier. They were jabbering excitedly about a pirate that the third grade class at their school had talked about, after their field trip to the Old North Church last year.

The little ruffians shoved in front of the Cape group, but left the private school kids alone. It seemed like there was something about the uniformed students that the South Boston class wanted nothing to do with. Maybe it was because some of the private school kids made fun of others in a superior sort of way. (But if asked, the South Boston kids would have easily admitted, with shy grins, that they often did the same thing themselves!)

In any case, the boys – Robert Hillman-Jones, Johnny Twofeathers and especially Frankie Sylvester – didn't like being pushed. Hillman-Jones pulled the boys together so they could plot how to get the upper hand with these toughies from the South End. Cape kids are used to the harsh elements and can be fierce and cunning when necessary. Like when defending themselves from being pushed around.

Robert had also overheard the talk of pirates, and he wanted to know more. Hillman-Jones was extremely interested in all things pirate. In fact, he had been to the Wydah Pirate Museum in Provincetown, and he'd visited the Pirate's Cove in Yarmouth last summer every chance he had.

Frankie was all for getting up on a high fence and landing on the Southies. Frankie preferred the direct approach. Hillman-Jones was more devious. He wanted to lock them up in the basement of the Old North Church. He'd heard there were tunnels under the church, and even better, they could freely search for the pirate's treasure when the other kids were out of the way.

"This is a *real* pirate's treasure," he assured the other boys. "It's not just some old story you hear."

He was convinced, even though all he had to go on was that the Southie kids had mentioned the words "pirate" and "Old North Church" and "underground den". But he was sure there was buried treasure to be found.

Ms. Finch had momentarily lost track of the boys. The perfumed air of spring and Xavier's long lashes had lulled her into a sense of romantic contentment.

But suddenly she noticed that the students had fallen far back. "Johnny Twofeathers, stay with the group!" she shouted.

Why she picked on Johnny made no sense, since Robert Hillman-Jones and Frankie Sylvester were the obvious troublemakers. In any case, the boys temporarily suspended the planning of "Operation Capture" and quickly caught up with the rest of the class.

They were now headed down Spring Street. The tour guide explained how this was once the water supply for the city. The Cape students looked at each other skeptically and had difficulty imagining how this narrow cobbled street surrounded by tall buildings was once a spring where people came for fresh water. Only a copper plaque on one wall remained to mark the spot.

But how odd! ElsBeth could see it as it once was, a beautiful place where sweet water and all the town gossip could be found. The little witch was having a hard time keeping past and present apart. There was so much history here. And in a funny way it seemed like it was all still happening now.

Soon they emerged from the dark street and passed the Paul Revere Mall. Lots of running took place once the space opened up, and the teachers began to have difficulty controlling their high-spirited young students.

Veronica and several of the girls were confused. "This doesn't look anything like the Cape Cod Mall. I don't see Nordstrom's or Abercrombie & Fitch. In fact, I don't see any stores at all!" complained Veronica.

Lisa Lee spoke up, "Different type of mall. 'Mall' also means a shaded place where people walk."

"Lisa, do you know everything?" Amy asked in wonder.

At the end of the mall on the right was the Old North Church.

The Cape boys started elbowing each other as they passed the word along. They were going to scare the South End kids. Then they were going to take off in search of pirate treasure.

Chapter XI
BENEATH THE OLD NORTH CHURCH

Somehow they would have to get into that basement. Johnny Twofeathers was sent to scout things out. Having no little training in this art, the young Wampanoag melted away unnoticed and silently circled the building. He soon found a hidden garden on the other side of the churchyard.

As he looked around he heard a rusty scraping noise and felt a cold, damp puff of air. He hid behind a tree just in time, and saw a skeletal hand inch out of an old door. Johnny swallowed his fear and continued to look as the hand became an arm, and finally a skinny, wrinkled, old man opened a door that was half below ground level.

The man looked around guiltily and then popped out, holding a cigarette that was soon lighted. The sneaky old fellow then headed away from the church, his secret safe, and Johnny relaxed. Luck was with the young scout – the sly smoker had left the cellar door slightly ajar.

Johnny scrambled back to his classmates, now neatly lined up for a tour of the building. The boys passed the word. One by one they silently dropped back and headed for the other side of the church and the basement door.

The remaining kids from all three schools poured into the church where the docents (knowledgeable guides – pronounced "doe sense") prepared to explain the fascinating history of the building.

The docent speaking this morning was a cheerful, red-haired girl named Beth. She began to tell the story of the beautiful carved angels decorating the upper level. They had been stolen by the famous pirate, Captain

Thomas Jacques, who had subsequently made a generous gift of them to the church.

Captain Thomas Jacques was considered by many to be a privateer, which Beth said was basically a pirate, but it was a pirate with a "letter of marque". A "letter of marque", she explained further, was an official piece of paper from the government that made it legal to steal from enemy ships.

This was a little confusing to most of the children, except those destined to be lawyers and politicians. To them this made perfect sense.

"Anyway," Beth continued, "recent research has discovered that Captain Jacques really was a true pirate. Granted, he wasn't just an *ordinary* pirate. He was a very *popular* pirate. And the church community gratefully accepted the lovely stolen angels, which have adorned its interior for all these years. And Captain Jacques was forgiven his many sins. And when he lived in Boston, he held a place of honor in the church! More interesting still, in his later years Captain Jacques had a role as a revolutionary and fought for freedom from an oppressive monarchy."

The boys, now lurking in the basement, could hear Beth's clear voice during her lecture, and though they weren't paying much attention to the history lesson, they loudly shushed each other the instant the word "pirate" was spoken.

Robert was making an attempt to organize them for action when suddenly footsteps were heard descending the staircase to the basement and the centuries-old burial place - the crypt.

There was not a lot of space in the basement so the boys scrambled around to find nooks and crannies in which to hide as best they could.

The knowledgeable Beth was leading a special tour for the private school kids. The exceptionally stylish girl, the one Veronica had objected to so much, walked past the dark recess where Hillman-Jones hid. He scrunched back further into his hidey-hole, but she smiled and nodded at him as she passed by.

Hillman-Jones coughed, "Drat," under his breath. This wasn't going according to plan. They wanted to lock up the South End boys, not these rich kids!

A noble looking boy – in fact, he was the very one with the turban who had admired Amy – walked by where Johnny Twofeathers was hidden. Two sets of almond-shaped brown eyes met in the dark. And some kind of recognition seemed to flash between the two.

Beth stopped in front of a small chamber and held up a wooden coffin cover. She told the children that in the old days a hole was cut out of the cover right above where the head of the "deceased" would be. This was just in case someone had made a mistake and the unfortunate person was not actually dead! At this, the children started looking around nervously for live "dead people".

Beth walked further into the poorly lit basement. She stopped where the body of Major John Pitcairn lay buried in the center of the basement. "Here may very well lie a restless spirit," Beth explained in hushed tones. "The wrong body was sent to England." The children looked at each other. This was a disturbing idea.

"At the bloody battle of Bunker Hill," Beth continued, "after trying to make peace with both sides, the colonials and the British troops, this beloved officer had fallen off his horse and was killed. There were a lot of dead and injured on both sides in the battle, and they were all brought to the church. Some of the fallen soldiers' bodies got mixed up in the confusion. It was war, after all.

"His family sent for him to be buried properly at Westminster Abbey in London, but another body was mistakenly sent to England. And his body remained here, despite formal protests and much argument from mother England."

The children were getting more nervous with this talk of restless spirits and misplaced bodies.

Beth turned a corner and passed along another wall. "Behind here is the saddest place. Here is where all the orphans are buried." Frankie was hiding right next to this wall, and he tried to move as far away as possible. Many shivers ran up and down spines as the kids filed past.

"Finally," Beth explained as she came to the area directly under the altar of the church above, "this thin plaster wall is all that separates us from the main underground burial chamber. And it's rumored that somewhere beyond the crypt, right on the other side of this wall, is a maze of caverns and tunnels that were used by smugglers in the old days. And these went right under the north end of the city and straight out to the ocean!"

As the pretty young docent spoke these fateful words, there was a deep rumble and a low cracking noise. And the plaster wall in front of them exploded in a cloud of swirling dust.

Before anyone had time to move, several black-masked figures rushed out and grabbed the turbaned boy. One of them pushed Beth, who was closest to the wall. She fell back and hit her head, and was knocked unconscious.

The masked men left her there, and quickly disappeared with the young boy back into the darkness of the crypt.

Chapter XII
KIDNAPPED

Robert Hillman-Jones and Johnny Twofeathers took off after them. Who knows why they took the kid – all Hillman-Jones could think of was they must be after the pirate treasure, which he had already claimed as his own. And there was no way they would get away with that! The treasure was *his*.

He and Johnny vanished into the shadows behind the wall. Frankie stumbled after them, followed by Nelson, who had thoughtfully taken care to sit Beth up – she had started to choke on the plaster dust. But once he saw she was breathing OK, he was off. Jimmy Miller picked up the rear, his backpack trailing his yellow slicker as he went.

Behind them the private school kids were in a panic. Strangely, though, if anyone had bothered to look, they would have seen their teacher, the one with the candy-red glasses, standing calmly by with a small satisfied grin.

Considering how quickly the kidnapping had happened, it was surprising that the mysterious Xavier had managed to plunge down the ancient staircase and shoot into the hole in the crypt wall merely seconds after the boys.

Ms. Finch, unwilling to part from the handsome Xavier, had dashed after him. But she had fallen a little behind and had lost sight of him on the long twisted stairwell. Of course, the curious Cape girls were right behind Ms. Finch, not knowing what was happening but sure that something must be up.

ElsBeth's head began to throb the minute her foot touched the basement floor, and hundreds of ghosts began to shout at her, trying to get her attention. But when she realized something was seriously amiss, she concentrated as hard as she could and was mostly able to block them out.

The little witch spotted the pretty private school girl standing close to the stairwell and said, "I'm ElsBeth. What happened here, anyway?"

The girl politely answered, "Hi, ElsBeth, I'm Violet. Someone grabbed Prince Abu Nadir and took him into the crypt. I think it's a kidnapping," she added seriously.

Lisa Lee was right behind ElsBeth and immediately grasped the situation. "Ransom! Abu Nadir is the most important prince to come out of the Arab Emirates in decades. He is royalty of two nations and worth incredible riches. Highly unusual for one so exalted to be without body guards," Lisa added thoughtfully.

ElsBeth couldn't believe Lisa knew all this. And what was even stranger was that her classmate was speaking. Again!

By now Veronica, Carmen and Amy had gathered round, too. Amy had overheard and her eyes glistened with tears. She'd only glanced at the prince, but he seemed like such a nice boy.

Veronica said, "Oh Amy, suck it up. Don't cry yet. ElsBeth will think of something."

ElsBeth was brought up sharp by this vote of confidence. She remembered her grandmother's words. Witches had duties. ElsBeth sure wished her grandmother were here right now to tell her exactly what she should do. But she knew she had to take *some* action. Now! No use wishing for things that couldn't be, especially when someone was in danger.

ElsBeth said to her friends, "OK, girls. We're going into the tunnel. Keep quiet. The first thing we do is find them."

ElsBeth narrowly avoided breaking the rule against using magic without supervision when she created an illusion of thick dust for Ms. Finch and the others. ElsBeth figured it wasn't *entirely* magic because she used some science, too. She magnetized the plaster dust particles that still hung in the air – and just gave them a little spin. And behind this cover, she and the girls also disappeared into the darkness of the crypt. None of the Cape girls noticed right away, but Violet had silently slipped along with them.

Luckily all the girls had on quiet shoes – even Amy's patent leathers and Veronica's hip-hop, rhinestone-studded sneakers made no noise. Of course, the innocent little "quiet spell" (those hardly count) that ElsBeth had cast didn't hurt.

"Hold hands!" Veronica hissed when the girls started to bump into each other in the darkness.

ElsBeth heard some squeaking ahead. "Thank goodness!" she said to herself. "I hear a bat."

Most people aren't too fond of the furry little flyers, but ElsBeth trusted them above all other creatures. After all, her familiar, Professor Badinoff, was a bat.

ElsBeth squeaked out a greeting in batspeak. "Which way did they go?" she quickly added.

"Which ones?" squeaked back the bat.

"What do you mean, 'which ones'?" ElsBeth replied. "We're trying to find the kidnapped prince."

"Oh, those ones went this way. Follow me, young witch," and the helpful bat was off to lead the way.

ElsBeth didn't have time to wonder who else was in the tunnel.

The bat headed out, squeaking loudly to guide her. Then ElsBeth used her own echo location, sending out little squeaks and perceiving where the walls were by the sound that came back. She began to "see" the walls around her almost as well as the bat did, though it was pitch dark. The other girls had no such ability, and they stumbled along holding hands. Only Lisa seemed steady on her feet. Her backpack was making odd small noises, but no one noticed in the tenseness of the moment.

Carmen stifled a scream every now and then when she thought she felt a mouse. Carmen was deathly afraid of the little brown creatures. But she was trying to be quiet, so she choked down the screams that desperately tried to escape each time she heard a noise.

The girls, truth be told, were terrified. But they trusted ElsBeth. And being Cape girls, the idea of letting someone capture a prince from another country was just not OK! So they trudged on, not wanting to think about what was up ahead.

Good question, though. What *was* up ahead? I'm afraid we'll soon find out.

The boys had regrouped and found they had several flashlights among them. Johnny Twofeathers had one he always carried in a special pocket of his backpack.

Not surprisingly Jimmy Miller had a heavy-duty, waterproof, crank-powered one. Jimmy's father was big on preparation for emergencies. "You can't be a commercial fisherman on the Cape without thinking ahead! You have to be ready for anything Father Neptune and Mother Nature can throw out at you," he always said.

And Frankie found that his mother had packed a goblin flashlight for him last Halloween that he'd never taken out of his backpack. The light was nestled under many empty candy wrappers. Frankie had been schooled not to trash the environment so he never threw a candy wrapper on the ground. Ever. And he ate a *lot* of candy! And since he made it a practice to never clean his backpack, there was a lot of paper in there! If the boys ever needed to build a fire, they were all set.

Johnny Twofeathers wanted to rescue the young boy first, but Robert Hillman-Jones was much more interested in striking out and finding the pirate booty and *then* searching for the kid, and this was causing some friction.

Hillman-Jones whispered reasonably, "Those men must be after the treasure, too. So we might as well try to beat them to it."

Johnny Twofeathers' argument won out, though, and the boys agreed to follow the kidnappers at a safe distance while they figured out a rescue plan. (But Robert Hillman-Jones was still determined to search for treasure as they went!) The boys moved as quietly as they could, through the muck of centuries, away from the crypt.

Behind some rusty iron grates set in the tunnel wall, unseen and unheard, a pair of ghostly gray eyes followed the progress of both the boys and the villains. And a haunting, low chuckle emerged from the owner of those eyes, accompanied by the lonely caw of a ghostly parrot perched on his shoulder.

The two groups stumbled along unaware that just on the other side of the mud and rock walls they touched were hidden chambers filled with gold, silver and glittering jewels: the bounty of many a daring adventure from long ago on the high seas.

After the fourth time past the same skeleton of an old rowboat, the leader of the black-clad kidnappers called a halt. He took off his infra-red goggles and flashed a small light on the map he carried in his vest pocket.

"Something's wrong," he grumbled, more to himself than to his men. "We should have been out by now." The more he studied the map, the more confused he became.

Chapter XIII
CAPE COD KIDS CAUGHT!

The boys, not realizing the kidnappers had stopped temporarily, almost ran straight into them. Fortunately Johnny Twofeathers spotted the light up ahead and grabbed Hillman-Jones just in time.

Frankie, Nelson and Jimmy all bumped into each other as they were brought up short. Nelson whispered, "What's up?"

Johnny made the silence sign and had the boys completely hushed before they gave themselves away.

Hillman-Jones leaned against the tunnel for a moment to catch his breath – and suddenly the rock wall behind him slipped back, silently opening up a chamber on their left. Robert stumbled in. He tried to grab onto Nelson to stop his fall, but Nelson just collapsed, tangling up both Frankie and Jimmy – and they all tumbled into the dark chamber. Johnny tried in vain to grab Jimmy to hold him back, but only succeeded in pulling the yellow slicker further out of Jimmy's backpack. Then Johnny lost his balance, too, and fell in on top of the others. And the rock slipped silently and firmly back into place.

Nelson panicked and began frantically pushing against the wall. Nelson wasn't too keen on small dark spaces. In fact, he hadn't been happy at all when he heard the docent, Beth, describing the crypt and people being buried alive.

"Buried alive!" he moaned. They were trapped underground. That was the same as being buried alive.

Nelson began to pound hysterically on the wall until Johnny grabbed his friend.

"Nelson, it's OK," Johnny spoke calmly in Nelson's ear. "There is fresh air in here. Do you feel it on your face?" Nelson stopped and felt the movement of cool, fresh air.

Johnny continued calming his friend. "We're going to be OK. Save your energy and be quiet. We don't need to let those guys know we're here, OK?"

Nelson started to relax. "Yeah. Right, Johnny. We've got to rescue the kid. Right," he said again, still nervous, but much calmer than before.

Johnny knew they were trapped. He just didn't want Nelson to know that.

It wasn't looking all that good for the Cape Cod boys, was it?

CARMEN MEETS A MOUSE OR A MOUSE MEETS CARMEN

Meanwhile, the girls moved ahead, unaware that the boys were also in the tunnels.

Veronica was *not* pleased that she'd fallen down and gotten her new clothes muddy. Amy was frightened for the mysterious young boy who seemed so nice. Violet was quietly following along, holding Amy's and Lisa's hands.

Carmen was being as brave as she could in the presence of probable mice everywhere! Lisa remained steady and analytical. Her backpack, however, seemed to be squirming even more than before.

ElsBeth was more focused now that they had distanced themselves from the crypt. But she had a funny feeling there was somebody . . . or something . . . else down here. She felt a presence nearby watching, but she knew she had to concentrate on the kidnapped boy. And she kept asking herself what she and her friends could do when they found him.

What indeed! There, farther down the tunnel right in front of them, she could just make out the echo of shapes clustered in the center of a cavern that opened up where several tunnels met.

And just then a real mouse ran across Carmen's red suede shoes and up her orange tights! The nervous second grader lost it! She began shrieking at the top of her lungs, "Help! A mouse!! A mouse!!!"

The girls froze.

The boys, locked behind the wall, heard the wail and altogether said, "Carmen!"

Johnny unnecessarily added, "Oh no. The girls are down here."

But worse yet, one by one, the black-clad figures turned. Two held the young prince tight, and the other three took off and grabbed the girls before they could even blink. One had Amy and Veronica and another held Carmen and Violet, while Carmen still shrieked – really loud! The biggest one grabbed ElsBeth and Lisa, legs kicking wildly, and hauled them over to the leader of the group.

"Well, well, well. What do we have here? A flock of little girls. What should we do with them?" he asked the prince in a heavy foreign accent.

"Should I dispose of them here, Prince?" the cruel man laughed.

The young royal stiffened.

"No. I think I'll bring them with us – they could come in handy," he said to his men. "If I know our young captive, his sense of honor will keep him in line the minute I threaten to touch a hair on one of their little heads. Hah, hah," he laughed at his clever little plan.

Things were *not* looking good. The boys were trapped. The girls captured. Ghosts all around. And a royal kidnapping. Boston was certainly quite a city – above *and* below street level.

Perhaps Hannah Goodspell had been right.

Chapter XIV
THE PIRATE IS PUSHED TOO FAR

The famous pirate, Captain Thomas Jacques, hadn't had anyone dare enter his smuggler's lair in ages. In fact, it had been so dull around the North End tunnels and caverns, ever since he'd scared away the Mafia, that the bored captain had settled in and taken a long nap. Actually, a very long nap.

He'd had some fun leading those common kidnappers in circles the last half hour, though. And locking up those pesky boys had been a treat. But now he was mad. You didn't take fair young maidens and kidnap them. It just wasn't done! It was against the rules of war, after all.

"These criminals are not going to get away with this," the dandy pirate declared. "Not in me smuggler's den! Besides, I don't like them getting that close to me treasure. . . . It's just not right!"

The pirate thoughtfully scratched his neatly combed and braided beard. The ghostly parrot on his shoulder squawked "Hear! Hear!" in agreement with his master's thoughts.

"Well, Percival," the pirate captain nodded to his fine feathered friend, "I don't want to trap them here. They don't look much like good company. But they do need to learn a lesson. Don't they, now!"

The pirate then counted off the important points of his personal philosophy.

"Number One - Ye don't mess with young misses."

"Number Two - Ye don't mess with a pirate."

"And Number Three - Most important of all, ye don't mess with *me* treasure!"

And with this said he roared mightily and materialized in full glory, right in front of the villains.

For some reason, maybe because he thought this was a mere genie, the lead kidnaper wasn't impressed. "What's this? Some pesky sprite from a bottle?"

Pirate Captain Thomas Jacques snarled back, "Insult me at yer peril, ye dusky villain! I'm no weak-willed spirit who was foolish enough to be stoppered in a bottle. I'm a proper pirate ghost, I am. Prepare to meet yer maker, ye pestilent landlubber!"

The pirate did a couple of fancy spins and swished his sword through the air.

The lead villain was still not impressed – he clearly wasn't familiar with the capabilities of a genuine, American pirate ghost. The other criminals, though, quaked in their boots.

The leader taunted, "You're a weak apparition if I ever saw one."

"What?" howled the pirate ghost, shocked at the man's total lack of fear. "Ye'll regret this, ye mortal!" he shouted.

The pirate swung his cutlass and whacked the villain with the flat of his sword on the foolish fellow's broad behind.

"Ow! That ghost's for real! Run!" And the big fellow was off as fast as his thick legs could carry him.

His men needed no further encouragement. The two holding the prince kept a firm grip on their prize, but the girls were dropped like so many sacks of grain. All except Amy, whose curly hair and frilly dress had gotten caught up in the gear of the kidnapper holding her. It was easier for him to run with her on his shoulder than to stop and try to untangle the little girl.

The tunnels under Boston's North End seemed to go on and on. But the young prince wasn't scared. He'd been schooled in ancient martial arts for all his young life. Fear was not something he would allow himself. What was the worst that could happen, after all? These bumbling men would attempt to ransom him and his father would lose a few millions. Or not. Something his family could afford in any case. The only thing that worried him was the young girl. He felt something tug at him when he heard the girl with blond curls sobbing quietly. He wouldn't want her to get hurt in all this.

Meanwhile, when the pirate had put his attention on scaring the kidnappers, the stone had rolled back from where the boys were trapped. Apparently the ghost could not long maintain more than one enchantment at a time. The boys rushed to where all the commotion was and were reunited with the girls.

The pirate stood still in the middle of the central cavern angrily muttering to himself. ElsBeth crept over next to Johnny Twofeathers. "Johnny, we've got to do something to save the prince and Amy."

Nelson came out of shock when he heard Amy's name. "Oh no! They've got Amy? What are we going to do?"

"We're going to get the treasure first. That's what." Robert Hillman-Jones butted in.

"In case you didn't notice, there is a pirate over there," Veronica added. "And it would be my guess that it's *his* treasure, and he looks pretty mean to me!"

And he did, too. With his long, red, curly hair and his silver sword and his gray ghost parrot, he was quite a sight.

"We need to get out of here," Violet whispered.

Veronica noticed Violet for the first time and said, "How did she get here?"

"It doesn't matter," Lisa Lee spoke up. "The kidnappers out there are afraid of the pirate. Maybe if we appeal to his sense of honor, we could get him to help."

ElsBeth, as the only witch present, recognized that the burden was on her to approach the pirate ghost. Alive or dead, she knew all creatures were tied by an unbreakable bond. ElsBeth's grandmother had several ghost friends. Some were friendly, and some . . . well, some were not so friendly. But she quickly decided not to dwell on that. She had to do *something*. The prince did seem like such a nice boy and Amy was one of her best friends forever.

Just then the bat flew by the young witch's ear and whispered, "Flattery, ElsBeth. You can win him over with flattery. And don't call him a pirate. He likes to think of himself as a privateer, and a patriot! His name is Captain Thomas Jacques," the bat added helpfully.

ElsBeth was still confused on this point. "What's the difference between a pirate and a privateer?" she asked. "They sound the same."

"Well, a pirate just takes what he wants from other ships. Stealing, you know. But a privateer has permission from his government to steal from an enemy ship. It's a fine legal point, to be sure. But as they say, 'All is fair in love and war,'" the clever bat added.

ElsBeth wasn't really sure what all this meant, but she got the point that the pirate liked to be called a privateer.

"Mr. Privateer, Captain." ElsBeth called out respectfully.

The pirate, deep in thought at that moment, turned toward ElsBeth with surprise on his ghostly face.

"You're not afraid of me, little girl?" he asked curiously.

"Well, sir, Mr. Privateer, sir, maybe I'm a little afraid, but those bad men took that nice prince and one of our best friends, and we need help to get them back. Can you help us, sir?" she added politely, remembering all the lessons her grandmother taught her about the importance of manners, particularly in sticky situations.

The pirate was even more surprised. Then understanding dawned. "The little one's a witch! Haven't seen one in Boston for centuries!" he said to himself. "She must be a brave one."

"Well, why not!" he muttered to his parrot and announced to the children. "It's been as boring as a one-sided game of chess down here for the last twenty years or so, ever since the Mafia stopped using my tunnels. I surely do need some adventure!" And he grinned from ear to ear. Unfortunately for the children, his grin was even scarier than when he was scowling before.

The captain growled at ElsBeth for good measure, "I'll help you on one condition. It's non-negotiable. You have to steal me a ship. I haven't been out to sea in too long and my sea legs are growing weak."

"Well . . . ah . . . OK," said ElsBeth. She wasn't too keen about stealing anything. Her grandmother had taught her right from wrong. She knew very well that taking things that didn't belong to you was wrong. But she figured they could return the ship when they were done and explain the situation, and all would eventually be forgiven – if they could only rescue their friends.

Veronica, suddenly brave, spoke out, "We can't steal a boat!"

Robert Hillman-Jones whispered, "Yes, we can, and then we can come back for the treasure."

Then Nelson surprised them all by boldly jumping up in front of the pirate and announcing, "We're wasting time. We need to rescue Amy!"

With a gleam in his eye, the ghostly captain slapped Nelson on the back. "That's the spirit, me bucko! Off we go!"

THE KIDNAPPERS ESCAPE AND
THE CHASE IS ON!

Up to that point the pirate had held an enchantment to keep the villains trapped in the seemingly endless tunnels under Boston's North End. But now that his attention was *thoroughly* distracted, that enchantment faded, too. And old granite steps and a weathered wooden door, held together with leather straps and rusty iron bars, appeared before the villains.

Finally seeing a way out, the leader yelled, "This way, men!" They scrambled into the blinding daylight, and found themselves right next to a wharf in Boston Harbor. Closely following them were the second graders, led by the pirate (or privateer, as he preferred).

The kidnappers had arranged for a getaway car, but that was on the other side of the city. They hadn't planned to end up here.

So when they saw the pirate burst through the door close on their heels – and now looking a little more real than ghostly – they jumped onto the deck of the nearest motoryacht. The men scrambled to untie the moorings, start the engine, and in less than a minute they were off – before the kids and the pirate had a chance to jump aboard.

Nearby sparkled a lovely wooden sailing boat. The pirate smiled. "There ye are, me lovely!" he purred, and took off for its gleaming decks.

A young couple in crisp white sailing outfits were stunned to see a large, sword-carrying pirate running full speed down their gangway. "Must be a Mardi Gras theme party," the woman said to the man.

But when the pirate pushed the man aside, that didn't seem so cute. "Now, now, my good man," the gentleman in white began to protest. "You must be drunk. Get off my boat this instant or I'll call the harbor master." And at that, the pirate threw the fellow and his stylish wife into the water!

Johnny Twofeathers grabbed two life rings and swung them down to the sputtering pair, while ElsBeth, Nelson, Frankie, Hillman-Jones, Jimmy, Carmen, Veronica, Violet and Lisa (with her noisy backpack), and finally the parrot (who'd fallen behind when the pirate made his mad dash for the gangway) all jumped aboard.

"Wow, I really didn't want to steal a boat. Do you think we'll get arrested?" asked ElsBeth.

Veronica, wise in the ways of the world answered, "Of course we will. It's stealing after all. We don't own it, do we? Now we're common criminals. The police will be after us in no time," she added darkly.

Veronica's words did not exactly put ElsBeth's already overactive conscience at ease.

The kidnappers hadn't seen the kids and pirate take the other boat. They were too busy trying to navigate the narrow channels marked by buoys that were the harbor's "streets".

And no one on either ship had noticed the large black cat who, at the last moment, also jumped aboard the pirate's newly claimed vessel. (Of course, the invisibility spell he had cast may have helped.)

Sylvanas had kept a magical eye out for the children, even as he was involved above ground in his own search for the answer to Hannah Goodspell's deteriorating state. He had perceived that ElsBeth was in some trouble down in the tunnels. But the cat wasn't big on being underground himself – too many spiders for his liking, and he had already used up most of his nine lives. So he had patiently watched for them, hoping they would pop up before he'd have to come to their rescue. (Of course, if things had gotten *really* out of hand, he would have been there like a shot, spiders or no spiders.)

Now that the kids were out of one dangerous situation, though clearly into a worse one, he decided he really *did* need to get involved. His research into Hannah's situation would have to wait. He leapt aboard. And it was a beautiful leap! He flew just above the water and landed softly in the canvas sail rolled up by the ship's railing. Unfortunately, he got a little tangled up in the ropes. And with all this exertion, the plump Sylvanas fell promptly into a deep sleep.

Johnny Twofeathers, the most level-headed in the group, began to take the pirate's directions and cast off all lines. At the same time Jimmy Miller was ordered to take the wheel. The sails were raised and the pretty little racing yacht was underway as slick as can be. Jimmy was right at home on this vessel, which wasn't too different from the boat his Uncle Tobias had. The pirate left navigation out of the harbor to the obviously capable Cape children and grabbed the spyglass attached to his belt. And with a practiced eye he watched as the kidnapper's ship came up to speed.

Unbeknownst to all, the mysterious Xavier had found his own small craft and joined in the pursuit. But to what end? Who was he anyway? Why was he here and what did the handsome stranger intend for all those involved?

Sea Chase

Chapter XV
TWO SHIPS AT SEA

Back on the sailing yacht the children noticed that their ship was christened the *Bon Adventure* and was based in South Yarmouth, not far from their own village. It looked like the Cape second graders were certainly off on an adventure, whether they wanted to be or not. And they could only hope it would be "bon" (which Lisa had patiently explained was the French word for "good").

The kidnappers managed to get past the harbor master in their ship, aptly named *The Jolliest Roger*, and were quickly out in open ocean. The leader was now calmly making plans to meet up with the men who'd ordered the kidnapping. But the others onboard the stolen vessel were pretty spooked after their close encounter with the pirate.

Speaking of the ghostly captain of the *Bon Adventure*, he'd found several flags stowed on board by the owners, who it seemed had a sense of humor, or at least knew how to put on a good party. The pirate chuckled to himself as he chose the black flag with the crossed swords, and chuckled harder when he pulled out a flag with an hourglass. He had Robert Hillman-Jones run them up the mast.

Pirate flags have special meanings, as most of the kids knew. The pirate had just notified any ship nearby that the *Bon Adventure* crew was "ready to fight" (the flag with the crossed swords) and that "time was running out" (the hourglass).

The parrot, who was beginning to get his natural colors back as he became caught up in the adventure, flew over to the furled sail where Sylvanas was sleeping, ever so peacefully, and the obnoxious bird started squawking loudly, "Stowaway! Stowaway! Overboard with the stowaway!"

Captain Thomas Jacques yelled back, "Quiet, you silly bird, and pay attention! The chase is on!"

As the *Bon Adventure* headed out to sea under the pirate's stern command and Jimmy Miller's steady helm (though he had to stand on a champagne crate to be able to see ahead), the rest of the kids huddled together to make their own plan. The situation didn't look too good. They were on a stolen ship, captained by a temperamental ghost pirate who was hundreds of years old, in pursuit of desperate and dangerous criminals.

"What could be next?" they wondered worriedly, as they tried to work out what to do.

ABOARD *THE JOLLIEST ROGER*

Out ahead in the open waters of Massachusetts Bay, *The Jolliest Roger* wasn't actually a very jolly ship at all. The villains were nervous. The plan to abduct Prince Abu was not exactly going smoothly. They were in a stolen ship. They had the small blond girl aboard, an added complication, and they had missed the rendezvous with their partners in crime back in Boston.

The leader looked out over the cold, gray water. Ahead was a large Coast Guard vessel, and the sight of a maritime police ship made his decision for him. "We're heading south," he told his men. "We'll take the ship to Cape Cod.

"It will be easy to hide in one of the ports there. Then we can hijack a plane from one of the well-equipped, little airports. Those small town chowderheads won't have the guts to refuse us a plane. And we'll be out of the country with millions in ransom!" He smiled widely, his gold front tooth gleaming, at the idea of all those millions!

THE BONNY *BON ADVENTURE*

Back on the pretty little yacht the children had "borrowed", another scary looking individual was smiling. Captain Thomas Jacques stood near the bow with Sir Percival, the parrot, perched proudly on his shoulder. The fearsome pirate ghost finally had a ship under his legs and another in his sights. Oh, it had been a long time since he had felt the wind on his face and had a prize in his glass!

They were not yet into the Bay and it was early in the chase, but he felt this would be a good contest. The other ship had more size and speed, but he could tell the captain wasn't much of a sailor. The craft had barely missed the marker buoys heading out of Boston Harbor.

And as the pirate surveyed the busy harbor, his eyes shined brightly. So many boats – so much wealth must be stored in those holds! It was hard to concentrate, but he took in a deep breath to calm himself and . . . picked up the biting smell of diesel fumes.

"Argh!" he barked. "What have the foul British gone and done? Three hundred years ago, the air smelled of ocean and fish. It was sweet in its own salty way," he added, contradicting himself.

"These pestilent sons-of-guns have messed up the very air!" he yelled angrily, causing Carmen and Violet to jump up and hug each other in fright.

ElsBeth knew what he was talking about. Grandmother had explained, "In the old days ships travelled all around the seven seas with only the winds and tides to power them. It's the fossil fuels people use that are messing up the water and air."

Grandmother told her, "The earth is a living thing and some substances are poisonous to the planet, just like certain things are poisonous to people or animals."

ElsBeth decided that after they rescued Amy and Prince Abu, she would work hard to heal the planet. After all, it wasn't like they could just take off and go somewhere else!

ElsBeth's virtuous thoughts were interrupted when the pirate shouted, "Hard right rudder, Jimmy, me boy!"

The pirate had noticed the Coast Guard patrol boat dead ahead, and decided they might arouse a bit too much interest – being piloted by an eight-year-old, captained by a ghost, and manned by a pack of second graders. (Smart move, Captain!)

Nelson was leaning well out over the bow, trying to catch sight of his dear Amy in the kidnapper's ship that was rapidly outdistancing them. And when Jimmy turned the wheel, Nelson was thrown overboard. Luckily Frankie Sylvester was near, and with quick reflexes he caught the heels of Nelson's sneakers as they flew by. Nelson hung upside down over the side of the ship, and Frankie teetered on the verge of going over himself, pulled forward by Nelson's momentum. But gravity finally won out – Frankie, big-boned as he was, had a solid, low center of gravity, which came in useful at times like these. And he pulled Nelson back in and dumped him on the deck.

Veronica came over, and instead of fretting over Nelson as Amy would have done, she unsympathetically remarked, "Nelson, we're on a rescue operation. It is no time for a swim!" And with that, she tossed her head and strode back to the stern where the children were gathered pow-wow style. The captain and Johnny Twofeathers were now working together on a plan.

Captain Thomas Jacques explained, "OK, the wind is steady. And I think the weather will hold. We need to let out all the sail."

Johnny added, "Yes, our fuel is low."

The Captain squinted, trying to understand what Johnny meant about "fuel" for the ship. "Quiet boy. As I was saying, their ship is faster, but they are the worst sailors ever a-sea. Right now they're heading toward Plymouth or Cape Cod. If we take advantage of the winds and currents we may have a chance of catching up with them before they land."

Johnny was not about to be ignored. "I don't think we should radio for help because they may get desperate and toss the prince and Amy overboard if they feel boxed in." Johnny, as usual, was thinking things through.

The captain again seemed blank about the "radio" and stared hard at Johnny, but Johnny stared right back, just as hard.

Lisa Lee was sitting quietly at the edge of the circle. Her backpack was squirming again, and seemed to be making funny noises – odd squeaks and clacks. Lisa glanced at her pack a little uncomfortably and pushed it behind her, then quietly added her own take on the situation. "They are probably going to try to steal a plane at one of the Cape airports."

They all looked at Lisa and realized she'd taken the whole situation into account and thought it through even further than Johnny Twofeathers. Their classmate was kind of like Sherlock Holmes. She just needed the smallest clue and she could piece the whole thing together. Maybe this came from all those puzzles she did. Anyway, Lisa was scary-smart and they were all happy she was on their team, even if she was a little strange at times.

The pirate now glared at Lisa, but she didn't pay any attention to him at all.

Lisa calmly added, "Our main concern has to be speed. We can save a lot of time cutting through some of the shallow waters once we get near the Cape. But they still out-power us in the open ocean." Lisa lowered her beautiful, slanted eyes toward ElsBeth, "We need a strong wind."

ElsBeth was on excellent terms with the North Wind as it happened. She'd done him a favor recently when he got in a tangle with a hurricane from Florida. The little witch had created a diversion with a simple enchantment under her grandmother's supervision, and helped him escape to the Gay Head cliffs of Martha's Vineyard, where he had hung low and managed to narrowly avoid being caught up and carried away by the storm.

She'd call in the favor now.

ElsBeth wasn't to do spells on her own, but there was no rule against talking to a friend. ElsBeth cast her perceptions wider and wider till she found him. At that moment he was up in Nova Scotia bedeviling a particularly annoying fishing fleet, one of the few still using nets that are dangerous to dolphins and whales.

The little witch caught the North Wind's attention by creating a small twister (not really a spell – just a matter of heating up some molecules and getting them racing around, an easy task for even a novice witch).

The North Wind immediately noticed the pretty little cyclone and came over to investigate.

ElsBeth sent a "whoosh" message, using the vibrations of the spinning molecules (a technique which is lots of fun, by the way, especially when you want to scare people on Halloween).

The North Wind understood the situation right away, and with a last blast of cold air that sent the lead fishing boat spinning around twice, he took off for Massachusetts Bay.

Meanwhile, the pirate had decided to take firm control of the vessel, though he kept looking nervously at Johnny and Lisa. He ordered the children about with lots of shouts and glares. The boys and girls pulled together to raise the sails – not an easy job for people mostly under four feet tall and with an increasing wind at their back.

The task was made even more difficult as the parrot, Sir Percival, had decided he needed to help supervise. He was not a pleasant taskmaster, and he criticized their efforts at every opportunity. Somewhere along the line he must have learned this method of command, but had never observed that it really wasn't very effective –

especially with second graders from Cape Cod, who would have done just fine if he'd left them alone!

To make matters worse, he squawked so loudly that he again woke Sylvanas from his cozy nap. Of course, Sylvanas would have woken anyway because he was wrapped up comfortably in one of the sails, and they were all now being raised and set.

But Sylvanas was none too happy to end his nap with the unpleasant sound of a bad-tempered, bossy, squawking parrot. The huge cat raked one paw lazily in the air, and in so doing caught the parrot's beak and held it shut, while blinking innocently. The parrot flapped his wings wildly – feathers flying everywhere.

In the excitement of dealing with the magical cat, Sir Percival's feathers had returned even more to their full and naturally bright yellows, greens, reds and blues. The children momentarily stopped their work and stared in wonder. (If they had looked closely they would have seen that the pirate's dull skin and clothes were becoming brighter, too, as the chase heated up.)

Eventually Sylvanas tired of holding Sir Percival in his paw and let go, and the parrot said some nasty things in response. "You gosh darned landlubber cat! You Felix Domesticus! You son of a barnacle toad!"

It was hard to understand how Sylvanas, clearly a cat, could be the son of a barnacle toad. In fact, no one was even sure what a barnacle toad was, except that it seemed unpleasant.

After this distracting spectacle, Nelson took the lead in getting the young crew back to task. "Veronica, pull that sail over! Johnny, help me here!" And soon the ship's crisp sails snapped out full in the wind.

And once ElsBeth explained the urgency of their situation in more detail, the North Wind began to blow his hardest. Jimmy Miller had to lash himself to the wheel to make sure he didn't blow away. And the others grabbed onto whatever was handy so they didn't fly overboard.

The Jolliest Roger was speeding away, fast out of sight, but with the wind picking up and filling its white sails like fat balloons, there was hope the *Bon Adventure* would not lose the faster vessel.

Captain Thomas Jacques, happier now that he'd had a chance to shout some orders, explained his plan. "If the little girl with the squirmy backpack is right and that's where the devils are headed, we can dance this nimble ship through the tricky waters off Cape Cod and gain on *The Jolliest Roger* even more."

As the pirate gave the worried classmates hope that they had a chance to rescue Amy and the prince, ElsBeth happened to look to the sky.

What she saw there was troubling. There was that familiar face she'd seen recently in the stormy sky at home. It was there now in the clouds just as clear as could be. Who was it? Why was it there? What did it mean?

If the little witch had looked behind her and seen the small boat skimming over the water toward them faster than any natural vessel could go, and had seen who was at the tiller, she may have had a clue.

ABU FIGHTS BACK

Back on *The Jolliest Roger*, the prince had demanded to speak to the leader of the kidnapping band. The prince was no fool. He had learned to be observant in his few years of life. In his part of the world a young royal had to become wise quickly to stay alive. He had to gain any advantage he could. And he could not let the pretty little blond girl come to harm. He had to take action, no matter the risk to himself. And he noticed that something about his captor seemed familiar.

"I say, don't I know you?" the young sovereign demanded in his best princely tone.

The large villain looked a little nervous, but this didn't stop him from a blustery response. "You'd better be thinking about how to stay alive, and not anything else, if you know what's good for you . . . and the little girl," he added, looking hard at Amy.

"You're a Bedouin. I recognize the accent. My cousin's clan speaks as you do!" The brave young prince was not to be side-tracked.

The kidnapper sneered back. "What do you know of the Bedouins, you pampered young pup?"

"I know they are a brave desert tribe led by a flawed man," the young boy answered with no hint of fear.

The villain looked as if he were about to strike his prisoner, and the prince saw his chance. He taunted the huge man once again. "My father's cousin is a coward, a man of no honor. That is why he wasn't chosen for the throne even though he was the eldest son of the eldest son."

The prince's words struck home. The giant turned purple with anger. He lost all control and he swung his arm to strike the eight-year-old.

The prince then saw the opportunity he was hoping for by making the man angry. He neatly slipped free of the brute restraining him and kicked the villain's Blackberry overboard.

The kidnapper made a desperate attempt to retrieve his precious instrument – without it he had no contact with his employer. And worse, he had no internet connection – no access to nautical charts, no data, nothing.

But he was too late. And he and the prince watched the device fall in a graceful loop into the choppy blue waves, casting a colorful rainbow spray before it disappeared altogether. Alongside a dolphin broke the surface, chattering away, sounding for all the world as if she were laughing at them.

The man took another swing at the boy, who easily avoided contact, but the young prince failed to notice the three men now at his back. They landed on him in a heap, and the brave prince was down.

The leader shook his head. He had instructions from the very man the prince had spoken of, his father's cousin. The boy was to be unharmed – if at all possible. The reward was much higher if they managed to keep him alive. And the tribal leader was a moody one. Who knew what would happen if he noticed bruises on his young relation? Best not to take a chance at being stirred to anger.

"Take the little blighter below," he growled at his men. "Get 'His Majesty' out of my sight before I'm tempted to do something I'll later regret."

Beneath her long blond curls Amy's clear blue eyes followed the prince as he was shoved below decks. What would they do to him? Amy shivered with cold and fright.

Chapter XVI
MS. FINCH TEAMS UP WITH BIG MAC

"When I get my hands on those children . . . I've never had a second grade class like this in all my years! What will I tell the parents? What will I tell Principal Titcomb? What will I tell the School Board?"

A new, and darker, thought struck the teacher. "What about my pension?"

Ms. Finch paced back and forth in the cold cellar of the Old North Church. Beth, the docent, was starting to come to. The teacher of the rowdy Southie children had, of necessity, with all the wrestling around her students loved to do, become an expert at first aid. She immediately covered the docent with her colorful Alpaca poncho to help with the shock. The Southie children, normally as unruly a group as you could find anywhere, were for once being quiet and respectful. It was beyond even their experience to witness a kidnapping and an entire second grade class disappearing in thin air.

They had rushed down the steps as soon as they'd heard the disturbance below, and had just caught a glimpse of a leg of the last Cape child going into the dark. Some of the brave youngsters had been quite ready to follow into the crypt and attempt a rescue, but their teacher had quickly put an end to that idea.

Over to the side, the private school students were huddled together and whispering loudly. Apparently some of them had been told about kidnappings. And they understood ransoms. Being from wealthy families, they faced quite different risks than the children from Boston's South End.

They looked to their teacher for guidance. His cold, cold blue eyes behind his candy-red glasses could not be reached, however. And the slight, cruel smile on his lips made the youngsters turn nervously away. Then he caught himself, and made a show of concern. His voice dripping with sympathy, he said, "Don't worry, children. I'm sure young Abu will be fine. The police will find him," he added. Though how this was to happen when no one had actually called the police was a bit of a mystery.

Finally one practical second grader whipped out his forbidden cell phone to make the call, but the teacher grabbed it out of the boy's hands. "Cell phones are not allowed to students. *I'll* take that, thank you!" and he pocketed the offending device.

The student tried to explain, "But no one has called the police yet. I was just trying to help."

The teacher pretended to be insulted. "Of course they've been called. I did it myself just a moment ago. You must not have noticed," he added, staring the young boy down.

Several students looked at each other, eyes wide. No one had seen or heard any such thing, and the children inched away from their teacher, who was acting weirder by the minute.

Even Ms. Finch felt that something was terribly "off", and found herself unconsciously backing up as far as she could until she was against the old plaster wall. Then she turned abruptly, took a few steps to her left, and quietly let herself out the back door to the garden at the side of the church. She knew her students. They were Cape Codders. They would somehow make it through this ordeal, and she needed to meet up with them when they did.

Ms. Finch would never admit it, but sometimes she had these flashes of intuition, and she had one of those now. It was not that she believed in the supernatural or magic in *any* form. But she found it always paid off to listen when she had "one of those feelings".

Soon she was dashing awkwardly down the pavement back toward Boston Commons, looking like some great, strange, gawky bird with her cape flapping behind. Ms. Finch pushed and shoved through the crowds of tourists, students, and even a few native Bostonians. And as she came to the swan boat pond she spotted her bus driver's athletic figure. He was sampling a jelly doughnut, sniffing it with profound pleasure, and taking large juicy bites.

She wasted no time.   "Come with me, Mr. MacSweeney! We are leaving right now!" This command was delivered in her best "don't mess with me, young man" voice, which always produced instant compliance.

The astonished MacSweeney dropped his exquisite doughnut on the ground – an occurrence, I assure you, which would never happen under normal circumstances.

"Where is the class?" he managed to ask.

Ms. Finch ignored his question and merely snapped, "Come on!" as she rushed headlong to the familiar yellow bus.

Mac hopped in behind her and was up the steps in one leap. The trusty engine coughed to life, and with a short squeal of the tires they sped through the park and entered the tangle of downtown Boston traffic, heading south toward the friendlier land of Cape Cod.

Chapter XVII
SHOALS AND ROCKS, TIDES AND CURRENTS

The little sailing yacht had barely stayed afloat rushing through the waters of Massachusetts Bay with the North Wind blowing at near-gale force behind it. But it still couldn't match the speed of *The Jolliest Roger* with its powerful diesel engines set to top speed.

Jimmy Miller had done his best, and quite good that was. If he were just a little taller he could probably be at the helm of a winning schooner in the Figawi Regatta, the annual sailboat race from Hyannis to Nantucket. Learning to navigate the challenging waters around the Cape and Nantucket Sound with his dad had been great training, and was likely to come in handy trying to catch up with these villains.

ElsBeth was racking her brains. Even with Jimmy's great skill, there was a good chance they would lose sight of the other vessel, which was even now receding to a small dot on the horizon. And if that happened, they'd never be able to find it with all the opportunities for escape along the difficult Cape Cod coastline.

The pirate edged over to ElsBeth and startled her by placing an icy hand on her shoulder. "Well, little witch, I've sailed many a worthy vessel and had the finest of pilots work in me crews. And I'll vow to ye our young helmsman could keep pace with the best of them. In fact, I wish I'd had the young bugger with me last time I was outrunning one of His Majesty's vessels on the High Seas," the pirate dandy added with a far-away smile.

But his encouraging words did nothing to help. What difference did it make if Jimmy was doing his best and they still lost their friends? ElsBeth was getting mad – really, she was frightened for Amy and Prince Abu, but the words came out like she was angry. "You're the pirate! I thought you were going to help!" The little witch was so upset she began to blame Captain Thomas Jacques for their situation.

The pirate was guilty of a lot of things, true enough, but he had nothing much to do with *this* state of affairs. He understood the witch's frustration, but he wasn't about to let her get away with being rude. "Well, well, little missy, first of all, I'm a privateer, not a pirate," he said pointedly. "And next, I'm yer elder, so ye'll treat me with respect! And finally, yer the witch! A captain can only make a vessel go as fast as the winds will take her. We've gotten every knot out of her that she can give us. If we can't go any faster, we need another solution." And he winked at ElsBeth.

"The nerve of him to wink when our friends are in danger of their lives!" she thought. Then suddenly the little witch got it. The pirate was telling her that if they couldn't go faster, the other ship needed to go slower.

ElsBeth thought deeply, "How can I slow them down? I've already got the North Wind pushing us as fast as he can. I'm not very good at getting the ocean to do anything. Grandmother hasn't taught me how to do that yet."

Then she noticed a beautiful sea bird circling the ship. And looked down and saw a dolphin jump out of the water. An idea was forming. ElsBeth knew she was good at communicating with creatures. It was her strongest skill. Somehow, maybe, the sea creatures could help her slow down that boat!

The dolphin perked up when ElsBeth came to that conclusion. She jumped high out of the water and splashed with a loud thwack. ElsBeth listened carefully to her series of clicks and clacks. And it wasn't a minute before she began to understand what was being said.

"I'm Desdemona, the adorable dolphin, at your service, young witch. I see you're in some distress," she clacked away sweetly. "I was at the ship up ahead and they tossed a gadget overboard. I think it was important. One of the men on the ship was so angry that he turned a bright shade of red! Would you like to see it?" she added cheerfully. It wasn't often the dolphin had a chance to speak with a witch, and Desdemona wanted to impress ElsBeth and make the most of this opportunity.

ElsBeth didn't see how it could help, but at this point she was glad for any assistance she might get. "Yes, please, Desdemona," she replied respectfully. Dolphins are intelligent and helpful. And ElsBeth knew they should be given every courtesy. So she was careful to use her best manners with the lovely creature.

The rest of the children were huddled in the back of the boat trying to stay warm while the North Wind's icy breath was on them. But the pirate looked on ElsBeth's conversation approvingly. And several other dolphins broke the surface of the blue-gray waters. One dolphin with a plump silver belly gracefully tossed a black instrument from the tip of her nose.

It landed on deck at the pirate's feet. He wasn't impressed. "What's that? Looks like a small block of black iron," he added disappointedly.

ElsBeth had seen one of these before. Robert Hillman-Jones's Uncle Preston had one. She hated to do it. Robert Hillman-Jones was such a know-it-all and a pest, but this time she needed his help. "Robert Hillman-Jones," she called.

Hillman-Jones looked up, surprised. He jogged to the bow where ElsBeth and the pirate stood looking at the object. "What's up, ElsBeth?"

"What's this for?" asked ElsBeth, getting right down to business.

"ElsBeth, don't you know anything? That's a Blackberry – a pretty good one, the latest model. My Uncle Preston has one just like it."

"It's all wet." Hillman-Jones pressed the buttons at a mad rate, but he couldn't get anything to happen.

"What do you use it for?" asked ElsBeth.

"Well, it's a phone, and a computer, and a camera, and an internet connection. Why?" Hillman-Jones was so curious he forgot to be sarcastic. "Is there a treasure map on it?"

"You mean you can access nautical charts with this?"

She had an idea. If the kidnappers were angry at losing this, maybe they needed it to guide them. And if they lost it, they'd have to rely on charts in the vessel. And everyone knows the Cape waters are always changing depths. The tides and storms cut new channels and fill in places, and even make new islands and sand bars. It was almost impossible to keep up with these changes on printed charts. She grew excited at the possibility. This could really slow the kidnappers down! The *Bon Adventure* would have a big advantage if the crew ahead had to rely on nautical charts even a year old.

Jimmy, on the other hand, knew exactly where all the shallow places and rocks were. He knew the currents and could navigate the difficult Cape waters. If they could only keep the other ship in sight, Jimmy could start to gain on them for sure, as soon as they got into Cape Cod Bay.

These were a lot of "ifs", still ElsBeth took heart. There was a chance they could catch up. But then what? Well, she wasn't going to think of that now.

ElsBeth had not been looking out to sea since she'd started talking with Hillman-Jones. Now her gaze swept the horizon.

"Oh no!" she cried. "They've gone out of sight!" ElsBeth, the pirate and Hillman-Jones just stared. What could they do now?

On *The Jolliest Roger* tensions were mounting. The sturdy ship had sped across Massachusetts Bay without incident. But fuel was being consumed at an alarming rate, and as they entered Cape Cod Bay, the villains realized they'd need to land before too long. And with no internet connection, they would have to rely on the few old charts on board.

"Curses, that little brat really messed us up when he kicked my Blackberry overboard." The head kidnapper was not the trusting sort, and no one else in his crew had been allowed even a cell phone. And, of course, they couldn't exactly call "May Day" or use the ship's radio for help. Being international criminals involved in the politically sensitive kidnapping of a Middle Eastern prince didn't allow for that option!

That the whole crew was made up of desert dwellers didn't make them the best sailors, either. At least one of the crew had a small talent with engines. He could get them running, and point the vessel in a general direction, but that Cape Cod coast didn't look all that easy to approach.

The Jolliest Roger had kept near the shore as it went by historic Plymouth, and then along the north side of the Cape. It quickly passed Sagamore, Sandwich, Barnstable's Sandy Neck, Dennis and Brewster. The ship continued easterly but now had to turn north. It was headed straight up toward the outermost Cape, which now appeared almost behind them.

For those unfamiliar, Cape Cod does a cute little curve-back upon itself, and the Outer Cape tip at Provincetown isn't all that far, as the crow flies, from the Upper Cape near the Sagamore Bridge. The foolish villains, who only felt safe when they were near dry land, had followed along the coast and ended up traveling much farther than they needed to.

As they passed Orleans and Wellfleet, and then the sands of Truro, the lighthouses made them more nervous. Lighthouses were only built where you had a dangerous coast and lots of shipwrecks. Even these criminals from the desert knew that!

Would the Cape Cod waters claim yet another ship? Would the sea swallow up Amy and the prince, as it had so many others? Would ElsBeth and her friends be able to rescue them in time? These questions and others will have to wait. For something is happening back on the *Bon Adventure*, and we need to check there now.

ElsBeth marched back and forth, ignoring Robert Hillman-Jones's steady stream of comments about treasure. Finally Captain Thomas Jacques grew tired of the greedy eight-year-old. "Get back, ye selfish little pirate," he snarled.

"In me day, we took treasure for our country or our families, or at least for the love of the game. Ye are just gold-hungry! What's the matter with ye, lad? There are far more important things than gold. There is freedom and honor and friendship, and best of all adventure. Ye need to learn to care about something worth fighting for. Something other than yeself," the pirate added sharply.

Hillman-Jones was stunned. *No one* talked to him like that. He stomped off sulkily toward the back of the deck, but he began to think about the pirate's stinging words. ElsBeth was so deep in thought she'd missed most of the prickly exchange between the pirate and her classmate, but she heard the part about caring for something worth fighting for, and she thought the pirate was right.

Some while later a circling osprey caught her eye as she was scanning the horizon once more, desperately hoping for a glimpse of the other ship.

The osprey had been calling to ElsBeth. Thaddeus Crane had sent out a general alert to watch for the young witch when he sensed serious trouble was brewing. After speaking with Persephone the coyote about Hannah Goodspell's strange behavior and ElsBeth's secretiveness, they'd agreed to keep an eye on both witches. Something was clearly wrong, and the animals wanted to help.

They decided that if ElsBeth were found in need, the animals would do their best to assist. After all, Hannah had come to their rescue more times than they could count. They owed the loveable old witch so much, the least they could do was watch out for her granddaughter.

So Oscar the Osprey had stayed with the boat as soon as he recognized ElsBeth aboard. And now ElsBeth, in turn, had noticed him.

He circled lower and lower on graceful sweeping spirals, at last calling out, "ElsBeth, what's happening? Is something wrong?"

ElsBeth instantly felt a burden lift from her shoulders. She wasn't alone. Her friends were here helping. The dolphins were nearby. Even the dangerous pirate seemed willing. And now her dear friend Oscar the Osprey had arrived.

"Oscar, Amy and a new friend have been kidnapped. They are on a power boat named *The Jolliest Roger*. We lost sight of it almost an hour ago, and we need to find it." The little witch was fighting back tears as she said the last.

"Don't worry, ElsBeth. If she's on the seven seas, I'll find her." And Oscar was off. He swooped low over ElsBeth, nearly knocking Sir Percival off his favorite perch on the captain's shoulder.

The parrot had fallen asleep as the ship had sailed farther and farther south. He woke in a fine panic when he saw the osprey seeming to dive straight at him and passing less than an inch from his beautiful tail feathers.

While asleep, the bird had reverted to his pale ghostly-gray color, but on waking in such a state of alarm, his feathers again turned striking reds, greens, yellows and blues.

All ruffled up now, he decided to find Sylvanas and pick another fight. It was always good to scare someone else when you were terrified – "made one feel better, it did," the funny bird muttered to itself, taking off in a flurry of color.

Sylvanas at that moment was lying on his back, all four feet straight in the air, his large belly rather comfortably balanced in between. He was purring contentedly and dreaming of golden jelly doughnuts. In his dream he was about to sink his teeth into a particularly tantalizing raspberry cream.

Suddenly a rude squawk woke him. Eyes still closed, a paw shot up and snatched the parrot's beak in mid-flight. Sir Percival had failed again.

When Sylvanas fell back asleep, his grip loosened and the parrot fled back to the safety of his captain's shoulder. He straightened his feathers and pretended that nothing at all had happened. Having observed the whole thing, the pirate smiled. His bad-tempered parrot seemed to have met his match.

Sir Percival, for his part, did not forgive the insults he'd suffered from Sylvanas. And he lapsed into a quiet song to cheer himself up:

> O pity me, this bird at sea,
> Who doesn't have a friend.
> From ghostly sea to ghostly sea,
> I sail on to the end.

> But what end can be for a ghostly me,
> Who doesn't have a friend?
> A lonely me on a lonely sea,
> I sail on to the end.

Rum-tum, that cat! That feline gnat!
I curse him to the end!
That lazy cat may win a spat
But I'll get him in the end!

Halloo! Hurray! All night and day
I'll fight him to the end!
The game is on, he is my pawn!
I'll get him in the end!

During Sir Percival's little episode, Oscar the Osprey had located *The Jolliest Roger* off the waters of Ptown (Provincetown, the outermost town of Cape Cod, for those not familiar with Cape-speak) and had reported his finding to ElsBeth.

With this vital information, ElsBeth decided it was time to work out a plan with the pirate and Johnny. She spoke to Johnny first as the captain didn't understand some things that were a little more modern than he, like radio and engines and that sort of thing. "Johnny, they are off Ptown. They may not have any communication except ship's radio, and navigation is probably by whatever charts they have aboard. What should we do?"

Without for a minute questioning how ElsBeth knew all this, Johnny quickly judged the situation. "Our speed is good, but we'll never catch them at this rate. That type of vessel will have used most of its fuel by now. Ptown is too well policed for landing, though they'd probably blend in fine with that colorful crowd," he added as an afterthought. "They'll be worried about being questioned by a harbor master wherever they land. My guess is they'll try to put in somewhere on the south side. They'll try to escape notice in one of the smaller ports. I say we take the canal and try to intercept them on the south coast of the Cape."

The pirate had been listening attentively while Johnny was speaking. "A bold plan, me boy! I like it. It will be hard to find the varmints, though. We'll have to count on luck, and we've practically no chance if we keep on following them like this. But wait a minute, what are ye saying about a canal? There's no canal across Cape Cod. I've sailed these waters more times than ye can count. I guarantee there's no short cut across this perilous spit of land!" he added, shaking his head at the absurd idea.

Just then they reached Sagamore Beach and the broad mouth of the Cape Cod Canal opened on their right.

"Blow me down! There *is* a canal, just like the little Indian boy said. I wouldn't have believed it if I hadna seen it with me own eyes!" The pirate slapped his leg and laughed with glee. "We'll get those buggers, now. Wait and see! Helmsman, hard to starboard. We're for the canal!"

The North Wind had been so intent on blowing to the south he almost missed the sharp right turn of the little vessel. But ElsBeth caught his attention and he quickly shifted to the west, blowing the sails full just as hard as before with barely a moment's slack.

(For weeks afterwards hikers and bikers on the canal paths would comment about the unnaturally strong and icy winds that had been blowing that day and that seemed to come out of nowhere. Joe, the Channel 5 News meteorologist, puzzled over, and could be heard to mumble to himself about, this phenomenon for days. He was used to funny New England weather, but this was ridiculous!)

They sped through the canal, then south again as fast as the steady North Wind could take them.

They raced by Falmouth on their left and then Wood's Hole at the southwest tip of the Cape, and soon they could see Martha's Vineyard in the distance. The whimsical gingerbread buildings of Oak Bluffs were just visible through the pirate's glass behind the twin lighthouses on the island's northern tip.

The perky little ship flew along the Cape's south shore, past the quaint village of Osterville and the busy port of Hyannis. They passed a racing sloop, and some of the children swore it was Ted Kennedy with his two Labradors aboard. Others said, "No, of course not. Congress is still in session. The senator wouldn't be out sailing yet."

They continued past the small fleets of Yarmouth, Dennisport, and Harwichport, and finally to Chatham. Monomoy Island was on the right, and beyond that the venerable whaling port of Nantucket.

But where was *The Jolliest Roger?* They felt they surely should have spotted it by now.

ElsBeth looked at Johnny and Johnny looked at the pirate. They shrugged their shoulders. The young Wampanoag and the little witch were out of ideas.

The pirate frowned, Sylvanas yawned. ElsBeth scanned the horizon. In the distance she saw the sleek, curved backs of a pod of whales breaking the surface. On a small rocky island she saw seals lazing in the sun. The air was filled with gulls and other birds. The dolphins still kept up with their little boat.

These were her friends. They could communicate with each other. Some of the whales or seals or even the gulls must have noticed *something*. That was it! She was a witch. She *could* do something!

ElsBeth skipped to the bow of the ship and leaned over the side. She began a series of sharp clicking sounds. "Desdemona, we've got to find that ship that tossed the little black box in the water," she clicked in perfect dolphin-speak.

Desdemona eagerly clicked back, "I knew you'd need our help. We don't usually go beyond Plymouth Bay, but we had a feeling we should stay with you through the canal."

The pretty mammal chattered with the other dolphins – a bit too fast for ElsBeth to follow. And the biggest one – with a dark fin and powerful chest muscles – took off in a flash.

"Dennison is going ahead to check with the whales. And Darling will find out what the seals have seen." The smallest, most graceful dolphin took off toward the nearest island.

"Dorcas will check with the sharks," she shivered. "He is very brave. If they are in these waters, we'll find them!" Desdemona clicked emphatically.

ElsBeth concentrated hard, hoping to hear back. But a persistent cry from above caught her attention.

And just as clear as could be, Silas, a black and white sea gull of enormous width, introduced himself.

"I say, there seems to be quite a lot of activity coming from this little boat. What goes on here?" the bird cried at the top of his lungs.

Silas was a pretty hip bird. He went to all the outdoor concerts on the Cape during the summer and just loved people and their music, particularly experimental jazz.

And he loved popcorn most of all! It was his favorite food hands down. Even better than fresh oysters. Yum! And everyone knows you can't get fresh popcorn from the ocean, so Silas tried to hang around people whenever possible.

Living by the water, ElsBeth had seen lots of gulls, but regrettably she'd never taken the time to get to know one on a first name basis. So she was a little shy with Silas at first. You see, seagulls don't have the best reputation.

Then she realized she'd never even actually met a gull personally, so how in the world could she judge them? ElsBeth now responded to Silas in a friendly way.

"Hello!" she shouted. "We do need help, if you would be so kind. Our friends have been captured and are aboard a ship called *The Jolliest Roger*. It sailed around Provincetown a couple hours ago, and we're trying to find it. Can you help?" she added hopefully.

Silas puffed up his big white belly in pride. He had never been asked for help before, and the idea intrigued him. And this was a witch! "We gulls have to watch out for other birds kidnapping our young," he responded sympathetically. "Of course, I'll help. In fact, all the gulls on the south coast will help!" he cried, warming to the subject. "Never let it be said that a gull won't help when someone's in need!"

The heavy bird had worked himself into an emotional frenzy and was off. ElsBeth soon heard his piercing cries to a swirl of gulls gathered on the beach.

Silas must have communicated the urgency effectively, because suddenly the air was filled with white wings headed north and south over the National Seashore – that breathtaking park created by President John F. Kennedy back in the '60's that runs along the whole east coast of the Outer Cape. Their cries were deafening even to those on the boat. The passionate Silas had them all stirred up!

The gulls hadn't been gone long, and ElsBeth had settled back into thinking about what else she could do, when suddenly Johnny ran up beside her.

"Look!" Johnny said, and pointed off the bow. Coming straight at them at top speed was the biggest whale any of them had ever seen. It appeared to have targeted the yacht, which was a mere fraction of its own size. The children ran to the rail.

"Drop the sail!" the pirate yelled. The experienced captain realized that if they were rammed at this speed the ship would shatter and no one would make it.

Hillman-Jones, in a rare moment of thinking of someone other than himself, began to pass out lifejackets, getting Frankie to help, too.

The children struggled into the adult-sized vests. There weren't enough. Hillman-Jones saw they were two short. He climbed out of his and passed it to ElsBeth, who put it on in stunned silence. Frankie gave his to Violet. The two boys looked at each other bravely as if to say goodbye forever, but they were too manly to voice this thought. . . . Would this be the end?

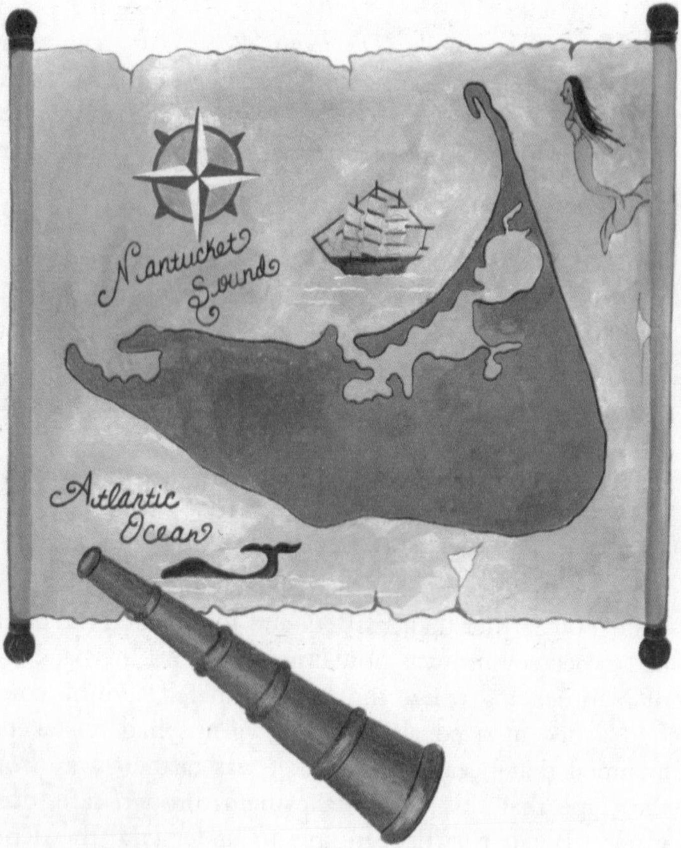
Nantucket
Sound
Atlantic
Ocean

Nantucket Sound

Chapter XVIII
ON THE FAR SIDE OF NANTUCKET ISLAND

Meanwhile *The Jolliest Roger* was recovering from a narrow escape – the perilous currents off the National Seashore had almost destroyed the kidnapper's ship. They were travelling south at low tide when one of the villains noticed a rock not two feet below the surface. He'd squealed like an eight-year-old girl who'd just seen a particularly large mouse. (Carmen sounded just like that!)

The other men had peered over the side, and two lost their breakfasts then and there – seriously upsetting some curious fish below at this nasty deposit in their crystal-clear Cape Cod waters.

The man at the helm, trying to avoid the hazard, had badly overcompensated and smashed one of the propellers into the shoal.

Nonetheless, the ship had actually managed to travel quite a bit farther than ElsBeth and Johnny and the pirate had expected, and was now limping toward the back end of Nantucket – where the lead villain felt sure he could find a decent-sized airfield. The villains had mistakenly assumed that because Nantucket was farther away from the Cape that this would take them through safe, deep water. But if they'd been able to understand the depth markings on the charts, they would have been terrified to see how close to disaster they were.

The waters of Nantucket Sound are actually extremely shallow except in the shipping lanes.

There is a Wampanoag legend that Gay Head, the spectacular cliffs of Martha's Vineyard, was the dwelling place of the great chief Moshup, a kind of Wampanoag giant. Moshup stepped onto the land that is now Nantucket Sound, making shallow places that filled in with puddles. And when he emptied his sand-filled moccasins, he created the islands of Martha's Vineyard and Nantucket.

Amy knew this legend about the Sound. But she couldn't think what was worse – to crash the ship or to get to shore and . . . who knows what.

So she kept quiet and prepared to swim.

She thought about the prince and how brave he was. And she thought about Nelson Hamm, and how his ears stuck out, and how his glasses slid down his nose, and how he always stood up for her no matter what. The two boys couldn't have looked more different, but at heart they were the same. They were both brave and true.

Amy decided if they ever got out of this mess, she would bake them both their favorite cookies. Amy was quite good at cookie baking. And she imagined the prince's pleased smile. Maybe he liked chocolate chip. Nelson, she knew, liked peanut butter. His ears would turn bright red if she made him some cookies, and he'd probably stutter, too. It would be totally sweet!

Amy's pleasant daydream was interrupted by a shout from below decks. The engine was sputtering and men began running up and down trying to figure out what was wrong.

The head villain climbed up on the top deck. "We're running out of fuel, men." He looked up and yelled at the helmsman, "Bring her in!"

Dead ahead was a natural cove with a huge mansion set well away from any other homes. "Looks like those rich people will have some company for supper," he laughed.

A WHALE OF A SITUATION

The huge, blunt, black head rushed relentlessly toward the bow of the bonny *Bon Adventure*.

"Blimey, I've never seen such a whale!" said the pirate. And if he weren't already a ghost, he would have been saying his prayers right then and there.

The parrot was hiding his face in the pirate's long hair – he didn't want to watch.

The kids were lined up on the far side of the boat, ready to jump and try to swim to shore.

Frankie Sylvester and Robert Hillman-Jones had rounded everybody up except for Jimmy Miller, who was holding hard to the helm. He wasn't about to abandon ship just yet. He figured if he timed it just right, he might be able to avoid collision at the last minute by turning the wheel hard and changing course.

ElsBeth grabbed Johnny Twofeathers's hand. "Johnny, have you ever seen a whale do that?"

"No. But I've heard stories about the days of the whale hunts. A whale would sometimes ram the boat if its calf had been taken."

ElsBeth stared at the huge mammal. Something didn't make sense. . . . Then she saw it! The whale's gigantic eye showed kindness and concern.

She understood! The whale was the fastest creature around and was trying to get to them as quickly as possible with the location of the other ship.

The whale wasn't going to ram them! ElsBeth started to giggle hysterically.

Johnny and the pirate looked at the little witch with concern. She was losing it. This happened sometimes. People reacted differently when faced with mortal danger. Robert Hillman-Jones got brave. Jimmy remained steady on, and ElsBeth . . . well . . . apparently she giggled.

The whale was almost upon them. Then Jimmy Miller jumped onto the wheel with his full weight – all seventy pounds of him. And the bonny *Bon Adventure* spun sharply, nearly capsizing as a result.

The whale stopped with a surprised look on her kind, but really big, features. ElsBeth looked in the whale's huge right eye that was now level with the top of the railing. In it she saw a reflection of *The Jolliest Roger* and the unmistakable coastline of Nantucket Island – former whaling capital, oddly enough! Then the gentle giant turned and sank below the surface, her job done.

ElsBeth wished she could properly acknowledge new acquaintance, but for now that would have to wait. "Someday," she promised herself, "we'll meet again and I'll properly thank you."

The children were chattering, "Did you see that?"

Robert Hillman-Jones was boasting how he ". . . wasn't afraid, not even for a minute."

Frankie, less gifted with words, merely added, "Me, too!"

Veronica for once was speechless. Lisa looked thoughtful, muttering something about "the millions of calories the whale must have burned going so fast," and, how "straight line swimming was abnormal behavior for right whales. . . ." Always analyzing the scientific nature of things was our Lisa.

ElsBeth tugged at the pirate's ghostly cloak. There was not a moment to lose. "We need to get to the south east side of Nantucket," she whispered. "Fast!"

Unlike the others, the pirate immediately understood about ElsBeth and the whale. He'd long since figured out the other children didn't know ElsBeth was a witch. He was used to the way many people were afraid of the supernatural. Being a ghost, he was the target of the worst kind of discrimination. Many people even said he didn't exist! That was the worst insult. Balderdash! Granted, he couldn't do many of the things he used to do when he had a proper body, but there *were* compensations. Now he could do *other* things even better!

In any case, he quickly set about giving orders to get the ship underway with all speed. He was rather enjoying this adventure.

"Helmsman Miller, back to the wheel and hard to starboard, compass heading thirty east by southeast! Seamen Hillman-Jones and Sylvester, hoist sails! Mr. Twofeathers, see about trimming to the wind!"

The pirate couldn't quite bring himself to ordering the girls. He hadn't grown up with the idea that girls could do much more than sewing and cooking, so he just turned his back on their expectant faces.

Veronica quickly understood they were being ignored and jumped in with instructions of her own. "Lisa, stow the life jackets! We don't want those stupid boys tripping on them. Carmen, wrap up the ropes and ties! Violet . . ." (Veronica didn't yet like Violet, but she decided the girl could probably do *something*.) "Violet, go see if Jimmy needs anything."

The girls got busy with Veronica's orders. Veronica could get cranky if you didn't do what she said.

Veronica looked over at ElsBeth and saw that her classmate was occupied with scouting the island, so she let her be and watched Hillman-Jones and Frankie as they scampered around to get the sails just right.

The North Wind was a little insulted when Jimmy had dropped the sails earlier, but when he noticed the whale heading dead at the little ship he forgave the young sailor. He didn't end up sulking as he sometimes did when he felt his efforts weren't being appreciated. Instead, he began to blow again for all he was worth. And Nantucket loomed closer by the minute.

The pirate carefully watched for shoals, but he needn't have worried. Jimmy was well aware of every shallow spot in this stretch of sea. Ever since he was a wee lad he'd heard stories of shipwrecks and lost souls. His great-aunt Millie loved to scare Jimmy and his cousins when no other adult was around to stop her. She'd pull out ancient nautical charts from the attic and point to the location of this wreck and that. She never tired of telling the terrible fates of olden vessels in the Sound and the dangers of the sea.

Fortunately Jimmy had been out to sea himself enough to know and respect these waters. But he wasn't afraid, despite Aunt Millie's best efforts. Her tales just added to his education is how he saw it.

Soon the *Bon Adventure* passed the northeast corner of the old whaling port. The pirate scouted with his brass spyglass. The children were tense with anticipation.

Would Amy and the prince be there? Would they be OK?
How could they rescue them?

THE NANTUCKET ESTATE

Not far to the south, *The Jolliest Roger* had struggled
into the small private harbor on the far side of the island.
The long dock there was an easy landing, but the
kidnappers had managed to head for it straight-on!

"Back up, you numbskull!" yelled the leader of the
group when he realized they were about to crash.

The helmsman was so relieved to be getting on dry
land again that he didn't realize you needed to ease in
slow alongside the dock, not aim at it headfirst. He
realized his error when his boss brought this to his
attention – with lots of yelling and bad words!

He was so shook up, though, that instead of reversing
he nervously pulled the wrong lever and accelerated.
Shouts and screams were drowned out by the crash when
they rammed the dock at a good clip.

Amy covered her eyes. She couldn't stand to see such
bad seamanship.

The now pitiful *Jolliest Roger* sat on top of the hundred
foot dock and was not about to go anywhere soon –
never mind the damaged prop and practically no fuel.

The villains nervously looked toward the mansion
across the once-manicured lawns that now sprouted
gangly weeds. There was no sound. It appeared no one
had been home to observe their less than graceful arrival.

The leader yelled at the helmsman, "Scout out the
house!"

The luckless man continued his streak of misfortune when he jumped to the dock, lost his footing, and slipped neatly into the drink. Shouting words not meant for young ears, the man scrambled onto the nearest dry planks, shaking and shivering like a happy Labrador. Though he was anything but happy!

All watched as the soaking wet crew member headed cautiously across the lawn toward the spooky mansion, wondering . . . would he make it? And was anybody home?

Chapter XIX
THE PIRATE SPOTS HIS PRIZE

"Oh, oh, my pretty, there ye are!" The pirate beamed brightly. Not only were the ocean blue, the air sweet, and a strong wind blowing, but there in his spyglass was the very ship they sought!

The children crowded round. They couldn't see the ship themselves, even with their sharp eyes. Nelson was nearly collapsing with relief, though. "Amy . . ." was all he sighed.

Johnny Twofeathers spoke up. "Maybe we can catch them by surprise."

"No!" squawked Robert Hillman-Jones. "I'm not afraid of any kidnappers." Robert obviously hadn't thought how they were going to free their classmate and the prince from some pretty scary-acting, criminal adults.

The pirate interrupted wisely. "We'll keep out of sight till the last minute and then sneak up on them. I know ye are all brave lads, but we've women aboard and we need to be careful."

At this comment both the boys and girls looked disgusted and went, "Ewww!" all at once.

Jimmy expertly slid the boat closer to shore where they would be able to approach without being spotted. "Good lad, Jimmy," called the pirate. "But ye're supposed to wait till the captain gives the order," he added a little crossly.

The children were now keyed up for action. Lisa was holding tight to her squirming backpack. Robert

Hillman-Jones noticed this. "What you got in there, Lisa, a cat or something?"

At this Sylvanas woke up and snarled, "Another cat on board?" Sylvanas did not like to share the spotlight!

Hillman-Jones playfully kicked at the backpack. Lisa screamed, "NO!" Suddenly the backpack flew open and out popped the horny head of a creature seen only in story books (and the occasional movie). It had yellow-orange eyes that seemed on fire, a long red tongue, and spikes up its back.

"My parents will kill me!" Lisa wailed, while desperately trying to stuff the little creature back inside.

Jimmy Miller was so surprised that he almost ran the ship aground on a sandbar, then tugged wildly at the wheel and pointed the trusty little boat out toward open sea again!

They'd gotten pretty near to *The Jolliest Roger* all the while. But when the bow of the *Bon Adventure* was no longer hidden by the shore, the little ship could be seen. And as luck would have it (or not), one of the villains was looking that way and shouted, "A ship!" which rang out loudly on both vessels.

There was nothing for it. The *Bon Adventure* was spotted. The element of surprise was gone, just like that.

Children scrambled. Villains scrambled. And the pirate watched steadily, considering a new plan.

Archery Aunts

Chapter XX
UNDER ATTACK

To make matters more confusing, arrows began to rain down on the kidnapper's vessel! These seemed to come from the widow's walk of the old mansion.

And just when it seemed things could not get worse, Lisa lost hold of the baby dragon. And the little spitfire was over the side of the boat.

Jimmy Miller headed the ship straight for *The Jolliest Roger*. Captain Thomas Jacques was about to order it anyway. The captain was none too pleased that once again his orders were executed before he had a chance to give them voice. You have to remember the pirate had been a long time without a chance to boss anyone around, and he really loved to hear his orders boom across the decks again. So Jimmy was not making the poor pirate pleased at all.

But he tried to be a sport about it. "Jimmy, me boy, good job!" he shouted. Though he couldn't keep a hint of resentment from his voice.

Nelson, initially stunned by the shower of arrows, now yelled out, "We're being attacked by Indians!"

Johnny Twofeathers did a double take. "I don't know of any Indians living in a mansion on Nantucket!" he yelled back.

"Look!" Veronica pointed to two elderly women dressed in clothes from the last century up on the widow's walk.

Violet looked up, "Oh, that's funny. They look just like pictures I've seen of my Uncle Melville's great-aunts,

Faith and Mercy. I've never met them. In fact, I thought they weren't alive anymore. But I heard they lived on a big old place on Nantucket. And, well, they were supposed to be a bit . . . eccentric. . . . And they used to be archery champions," she added in a confused tone of voice.

"Wow!" Veronica was impressed. "Archery champions! Wow!" It took a lot to impress Veronica, but it appeared that Violet had managed.

Nelson was flailing around and bumped into Veronica. "We've got to do something! Amy's on board that ship. They might hurt her."

Despite the commotion, the North Wind hadn't let up on his near-gale force blow. And Jimmy was neatly steering the little yacht toward the damaged wharf at full speed.

And unseen by all but the parrot, who could only squawk he was so agitated, another small boat continued to skim just above the surface of Nantucket Sound, rapidly approaching all the action. The handsome fellow at the tiller looked for all the world like a young corporate executive on holiday. Of course, he didn't look entirely real or solid, though. He shimmered a bit, which is what got the parrot squawking.

As the *Bon Adventure* bore down on what was left of the wharf, the pirate yelled, "Hard to port!" and he then leapt the last five feet, touching down on the very edge of the now rickety wharf, and holding on just by the curled toes of his leather boots.

Cutlass outstretched, he stormed down the wooden planks, hair streaming behind, and the ghost parrot flapping loyally at his side.

"Arahh, ye villains!" he shouted. "Prepare to meet yer maker!"

Sizing up the situation – arrows raining down, a dead pirate running headlong at them, ship high and dry on top of the dock – the head villain knew his only hope was to use the hostages.

Running as if his life depended on it, which it probably did, he grabbed little Amy and was below decks in two winks, the rest of his men quickly following. That is, all except for the wet crew member, who had reached the mansion's front porch just as the arrows began to fly. And Amy was shoved in with the prince who'd been locked in the hold earlier.

Nelson, catching a glimpse of Amy's blond curls, and realizing that they were on a course to ram the other boat, yelled frantically, "Back, Jimmy! Take her back!"

Jimmy, seeing that the captain had disembarked and realizing *he* was now captain, took quick action to bring the little boat around just in time.

ElsBeth caught the North Wind's attention, gave him a nod and a wave, and let him know he was off-duty. He'd need at least a week to recover from all that intense blowing. He drifted off deflated, but proud to have been of service to Hannah Goodspell's granddaughter!

Meanwhile, Jimmy brought the *Bon Adventure* to a perfect stop, just kissing the side of the wharf as she came alongside.

ElsBeth, Nelson and Johnny jumped onto the dock and were immediately stopped short by the vision of the pirate stomping along the top deck of *The Jolliest Roger*.

Captain Thomas Jacques strutted back and forth yelling, "Ye lily-livered cowards, hiding behind a young girl's skirts." The pirate's voice rose in volume with each word, and he thrust his cutlass at each breath. The sword wasn't really hitting anything, but it seemed to make the pirate feel better to be taking bold action.

ElsBeth noticed a small open window on the side of the ship, and without further thought swung herself through, just like on the monkey bars at school, and her slight form disappeared into the darkness below. Johnny thought this was foolish, and he tried to grab her as she flew in, but missed.

ElsBeth landed below decks. Fortunately it was a soft landing. Unfortunately it was soft because she landed right on top of one of the kidnappers.

Sylvanas was not too pleased about all the wetness around him. After all, this was the ocean, and he was a cat, and the two don't mix. So he'd slept through almost everything up until now. But the minute ElsBeth got into the hands of the kidnappers, he was up and away! He flew through another small window in the side of the ship and let out a bloodcurdling screech – scaring everyone, including the two old ladies with the bows and arrows up at the mansion.

Nelson was pounding on the hatch.

The kidnappers were yelling, "Get back or we'll hurt the girls."

The pirate was stamping.

Every once in a while a random arrow landed.

What would happen? It was a Mexican standoff to end all standoffs (whatever that is). And no one moved an inch when two golden-orange eyeballs below a couple of funny-looking horns appeared at the window Sylvanas had just jumped through. The baby dragon had bumbled its way over to see what all the noise was. Dragons are terribly curious.

Lisa cried out, "Ling Ling, you're okay!" The little dragon was so overjoyed to see his friend that steam started coming out his ears and soon large flames were shooting out his mouth!

He'd been wolfing down banana pomegranate granola bars all day, which Lisa had left for him in her backpack, and suddenly it was all too much! He tooted!

A dragon toot is an experience you want to avoid at all costs! It is stinky beyond words. Think of smelly feet, rotten eggs, baby vomit and dog dodo all mixed up, and you'll have a faint impression of what a real dragon toot is like.

Everyone on deck caught a whiff and there were choking and retching noises all over. Even Sylvanas, known for his iron stomach, got sick. It was horrible.

And worse, Ling Ling tooted with so much force he was propelled up onto *The Jolliest Roger's* deck. The charts had been left rolled up in a corner, and that was exactly where the baby dragon landed. His fiery dragon breath caused a neat little bonfire, which would have been perfect for toasting marshmallows in other circumstances, but fueled by the tooting gases, the blaze rapidly spread out of control!

"Grab the prince!" the villain yelled to one of his mates. "And hold onto those two," he added, pointing his chin toward ElsBeth and Amy.

"Back off!" he shouted. "We've got the kids!" The pirate and children on deck backed up a step.

Out of the hatch appeared a villain, face blackened with smoke, then another, and another. Soon all were on deck, and a staring contest began.

But this was soon broken by a shout from the top of the mansion. "I've got the house secured!" The wet villain was on the widow's walk, holding the two aunts with their hands bound together.

Tumbling and flaming and tooting loudly, little Ling Ling rose up over the deck. There were spontaneous yells of, "Ohhh!", "Yuck!", "Arw!" and "Peew!" at the stinky little flying fellow. But Lisa couldn't have been happier.

The head kidnapper only stopped for a moment and yelled again, "Back off! We're taking the prince and the two girls. Anyone makes a move, they're toast!"

The pirate and children moved back again. But flames and smoke were everywhere. They were all going to have to get off soon or end up as burnt toast indeed!

They watched helplessly as the kidnappers pulled Amy, the prince and ElsBeth toward the dock.

But they finally noticed the little boat which had been discretely following the whole way from Boston. They watched it slide silently up behind all the commotion. And the handsome Xavier jumped lightly onto the deck behind the villain holding ElsBeth.

"Kindly unhand my cousin. Right now, if you please!" His voice was low with menace. Xavier had a fancy dueling pistol in his hand, cocked and ready.

ElsBeth twisted around and glared, "I'm not your cousin!"

Xavier ignored the little witch and repeated himself, not louder, but more menacingly still. "Now, I said."

The head villain pushed Amy against Xavier, who lost his footing for a moment. Nelson dived to rescue Amy.

Sylvanas streaked up the hatchway and pounced on the man who still held ElsBeth. Lisa Lee let out a piercing scream and started doing a mix of Judo, Tai Kwon Do and some other advanced martial arts moves, all the while looking like a small extra in the movie *Crouching Tiger, Hidden Dragon*. And speaking of hidden dragons, the no longer hidden Ling Ling devotedly followed Lisa everywhere, tooting and flaming his way across the deck.

Johnny Twofeathers and Robert Hillman-Jones joined hands and tripped the kidnapper who was trying to flee with the prince. Abu, finally free, gave them a quick smile and jumped into the fight.

The pirate stomped over and growled, "This one is mine!" He grabbed the lead kidnapper by his hair and proceeded to verbally abuse him with the best pirate insults he could muster!

The Dreaded Dragon

Chapter XXI
THE YELLOW BUS ARRIVES

On the opposite side of the estate, unseen by all involved, the yellow bus rumbled up the long, overgrown, cobblestone drive.

Ms. Finch, despite her usual firmly logical leanings, had gone all the way with her intuition this time. The teacher had bullied Big Mac into boarding the high speed ferry to the island. Truth was that Big Mac wasn't afraid of anything in this world – except Ms. Finch. He had meekly followed all the teacher's outrageous instructions.

Once they arrived at the mansion's wrought iron gates he immediately spotted the two damsels in distress – at least from a distance they appeared to be damsels – who were now being held at the edge of the widow's walk by the soaking wet and still shivering villain.

Mac jumped out of the bus and he shimmied up a copper drain pipe, with a ceremonial sword between his teeth. (He used this for his Irish sword dancing exhibitions and always kept one hidden, but handy, under the driver's seat of his bus, in case of emergency.) He promptly subdued the wet fellow, who at this point seemed overjoyed to be captured.

Anything to get away from the two old maids who'd been badgering him to death with all kinds of unpleasant threats like, "We'll tell your mother on you." "What's a nice boy like you doing breaking in on two sweet little old ladies?" And so on. The "sweet little old ladies" seemed to have conveniently forgotten that they had been the first to attack with a thunderstorm of arrows just a few minutes before.

Big Mac, with one swoop of his brilliant sword, neatly cut the two ladies loose. They now chattered away even more than before, if that were possible, and enthusiastically led Big Mac and the soggy captive down three grand flights of stairs to a kitchen big enough to roller-skate in.

Mercy, the eldest twin (by two minutes) announced, "Our hero looks like a man who likes jelly doughnuts! Let's make him some."

"Yes, dear," her sister, Faith, readily agreed, "We must properly thank the young fellow. Excellent sword play! Absolutely top-rate!" she gushed. "I'll get right on it."

Big Mac settled in comfortably at the head of the table, an eye on his shivery captive, while the two old girls began.

Outside, Ms. Finch sat down on a granite bench and closed her eyes. She had a blinding headache, something which always seemed to follow her bouts of intuition. She laid her head back and soon dozed off in the late afternoon sun.

On the shore side of the estate, *The Jolliest Roger* was now in full flame.

The *Bon Adventure*, however, had been pulled over to a nearby dock by the ever-alert Jimmy Miller. It now sat safely out of the way of the billowing smoke and fire.

The fighting had stopped, the dragon was now calmed and had been placed lovingly in the backpack again, and things were settling down.

With the kidnappers now in hand, the pirate announced he would sail the *Bon Adventure* back to Boston harbor, manned by his new crew, the villains. The children tried to talk him out of this. They were afraid the bad men would mutiny and turn on their new friend, Captain Thomas Jacques.

"I've most usually had at least one or two villains in me command in any ship I've captained. And I learned from me hero and fellow privateer, Billy Bowlegs – who also suffered accusations that he was a pirate! – it's the nature of the seafaring life. I've always found a few months at sea good for reflection – brings a man to his senses – clears his head – heals his soul. Besides, these men are the absolute worst sailors I've ever set me eyes on. And I haven't had a good challenge since I fought for democracy back in the 1700's. It's about time I did something interesting for a change. Turning them into a proper crew could be the greatest challenge of me long and amazing career," he added modestly.

"Besides, the salt air smells good to me and the sun feels nice," he added with a twinkle in his gray-blue eyes. "And I've a feeling there's treasure to be found around these waters – and I'm just the ghost to do it!"

That worried ElsBeth. She felt responsible for the safe return of the little ship they had "borrowed." "You're going to take the boat back to the rightful owners, aren't you?" she quizzed him.

The pirate glared a ghostly gray eye at the little witch.

"Sir," she added in a very small voice.

"Well, don't ye be worrying too much, missy. I'm sure this fine craft will find its way back to its owners . . . in due course," he replied mysteriously.

143

The children looked a little concerned. No one dared say anything. Except Robert Hillman-Jones.

"If it's treasure you're after, I'm your man!" And he stepped right up to the imposing pirate.

"Well, me boyo, I'm a man of letters, meself. And after you finish school, I might consider taking ye on. Ye started out a greedy little hooligan, but ye showed some backbone when things got rough back there."

Robert puffed out his chest. The pirate had noticed when Robert had been brave in the face of the whale heading straight for their ship.

"But I wanna come now," Robert whined in his poor little rich kid voice, which always worked with his parents.

"None of that sissy talk, young mister! Ye'll come when ye're ready and not a moment sooner, I say!" The pirate was considerably more effective than Robert's parents, and Robert reluctantly dropped the subject. He wasn't too happy about being called a sissy, especially in front of the girls.

The children were sad at the thought of leaving Captain Thomas Jacques. In one short day they had grown quite attached to the famous ghost. And truth be told, the pirate was a little sad, too. A small tear glistened in his ghostly eye.

There would have been an emotional group hug if at that very moment Ms. Finch, having woken up from her nap, hadn't wandered to the mansion's shore, holding her head in her hands as if it were about to burst, muttering, "I know those children are around here somewhere."

The wily pirate saw his exit opportunity. He corralled the villains at sword point, tossed off the bowline that Jimmy Miller had so neatly set, and slipped quietly off to sea in an unnatural fog that had conveniently just moved in. The *Bon Adventure* disappeared in moments, seeping into the gray-on-gray of water and sky.

The children now had a new challenge to face. There was Ms. Finch, and boy was she going to be mad – on so many levels!

ElsBeth was about to step forward and take the blame for their wandering off the Freedom Trail. (Witches are trained early to take responsibility for their actions.) But her foot suddenly stuck. And the mysterious Xavier stepped lightly across the lawn, motioning to the children behind his back to be silent. "Elvira, delightful to see you again! How's the head? Sit here with me a moment in the shade."

The dazed teacher looked up at the handsome Xavier and promptly forgot her headache, and everything else. Her beady black eyes gazed into his deep blue ones.

"My dear, you look chilled to the bone. Here, take my sweater." He neatly turned the teacher away and gently wrapped her up in his thick, cotton, cable knit, conveniently hiding the children who silently passed behind him.

But when Frankie got around the corner of the mansion and saw the bus, he let out a yelp. And the big-boned boy raced as fast as he could. In that beloved vehicle was his lunch box. There'd been so much excitement he hadn't thought about food . . . much . . . all day. But now that things had quieted down, his stomach was making scary, nasty, gurgling noises. Frankie was up the steps and into his peanut butter and jelly sandwiches, stuffing them down with both fists faster than the eye could easily follow (if you were actually brave enough to watch Frankie eating – few were).

Ms. Finch heard Frankie's excited cry and even Xavier couldn't distract her further. She caught a glimpse of ElsBeth and stomped over to the drive, all puffed up and looking ready to explode. There was something about that girl that drove the teacher absolutely mad!

But Xavier caught up with the testy Ms. Finch. "Elvira, surely we shouldn't make a fuss. I'm certain the children will say nothing of what happened today. Which is really best under the circumstances, don't you agree?"

It didn't take long for the teacher to imagine what the parents would say if they found out their children had been lost under the Old North Church, and had been alone on the open ocean and out of the teacher's sight all day. Particularly Robert Hillman-Jones's parents – there were lots of lawyers in that family. Never mind what the principal, Dr. Titcomb, would say, and the School Board. She pictured worsening scenarios of no promotion, no opportunity to be the theater coach . . . ever . . . and darkest of all – no pension.

Yes, Xavier was right, best to pretend nothing was amiss. If they headed back now, they could be home before it was too late. And they could blame their tardiness on the Boston rush hour traffic. Little wheels whirred in her little mind as she followed this thought.

"On the bus, children! Chop, chop! And Lisa, get that backpack cleaned out. It smells!" she added as she passed the offending piece of luggage.

The children marched aboard quietly. They were actually pretty tuckered out after the events of the day.

"Where is Mr. MacSweeney?" the teacher asked, looking all over for the daring driver.

"Oh, I'll get him." Xavier leapt up on the broken down porch and found his way to the enormous kitchen, which wasn't difficult as it was now emitting the heavenly scent of fresh beach plum jelly doughnuts.

He found Big Mac seated at the head of a long table made of some exotic wood and set with crystal bowls of fruit and silver serving dishes. Mac looked like a miniature king of old. A huge platter of doughnuts was piled high in front of him, next to a steaming latte in a matching mug. His mouth was wide for his first bite.

"Sorry, my friend," Xavier said sympathetically. "I'm afraid there's no time for that now. We must be off."

The dear old ladies were upset at losing their little hero. Actually, he was just their size, and they'd quickly adopted him. They were particularly thrilled when he'd given them a brief sword dancing demonstration while the doughnuts were being prepared.

However, on seeing Xavier's determined look, they surrendered their new friend and pushed the still wet villain into Mac's chair. "Here dear, you'll like a fresh jelly doughnut." They fortunately had a ready substitute to dote on.

The confused and frozen criminal had no strength to object, and those doughnuts did smell great. All he could manage was to meekly ask, "Could I have a cup of chamomile tea, please?"

"Of course, dear. It won't be a minute."

Xavier figured the thug was on his own, and would have no chance against those dear little ladies. They'd have him civilized in no time.

On the big yellow bus Ms. Finch was doing the final head count and came up with two too many.

Veronica's quick thinking saved the day. "Violet's staying overnight with me, and Prince Abu is staying with Johnny Twofeathers." The resourceful girl spoke convincingly.

Ms. Finch couldn't really come up with an argument for this, so she closed her roll book and turned around saying, "We're all set then, Mr. MacSweeney. Let's head back home. If we are quick enough, we should just be able to catch the late afternoon ferry."

As the bus spun out of the drive, Violet looked over to Veronica, who was now intentionally looking away. "Thanks. I wasn't sure about spending a night with my great-great-aunts. From what I've heard, nobody in the family ever went there if they could avoid it. They seem nice enough, but they're a little odd. And I think it would be harder to explain how I ended up on Nantucket Island. It should be easier to come up with an excuse for a sleepover at your house." The pretty little girl looked relieved.

Toward the back of the bus Prince Abu was equally happy to be going back with Johnny. He already felt close to the Native American boy. "Sometimes you meet a brother," he said to Johnny, "and feel you will be friends ever after."

Johnny nodded, knowing exactly what he meant.

In the middle of the bus a confused ElsBeth kept looking back and forth between Lisa Lee and Xavier. There were some things going on she just didn't understand. She'd of course heard of dragons and knew they were real, or at least had been at one time. She didn't know that any still existed. She thought they were all extinct, like the dinosaurs. She was going to have to ask Grandmother about this. And Lisa seemed different around Ling Ling. She actually spoke! Could it be that the little creature made Lisa feel more confident around people somehow? There was a lot to think about.

"And Xavier says he's my cousin," ElsBeth thought to herself. "What could he mean? Grandmother won't talk much about the family. She says it's still too painful. And she's all fuddled now. How will I ever understand?"

The little witch felt about to cry.

At that moment Xavier turned around from his seat in the front. He caught her eye and smiled. ElsBeth didn't quite understand, but she felt better, and not so alone.

Almost everyone on the bus was happy. Jimmy Miller had sailed a boat pretty much all by himself. He'd never sailed before without his father's watchful eye on him. In his mind he was reliving the perfect docking over and over, smiling happily to himself.

Frankie, too, was happy. He was always happy to be with his friends, and he finally had a chance to get to his lunch. Best of all, his mother had packed a quarter of an apple pie, his very favorite, just for him. He patted his round belly and let up a big satisfied burp.

"Ohh!" said Veronica, "Don't do that! It's rude!"

Veronica was happy because she had a chance to show Violet some of the jewelry her mom designed and Violet thought it was beautiful. Finally someone to share her love of fashion with! And it turned out that Violet's family had a summer cottage in Chatham and stayed on the Cape every summer. They'd have a chance to go shopping together in just a month. This was going to be great!

Amy and Nelson were happily seated together. Not looking at each other, of course. Anything but! But still happy to be close.

Hillman-Jones had his eyes closed and was daydreaming about meeting up with Captain Thomas Jacques again. He'd show that pirate he knew his "letters", whatever that meant. (Many years later, Robert Hillman-Jones would be reading an old novel that mentioned "a man of letters" as someone well-educated, and he would laugh out loud at his earlier self.) Robert was sure he'd find more treasure someday than that pirate ever imagined. (Which was actually the case, but that is well in the future.)

Even Ms. Finch seemed to be enjoying herself. She had begun a fascinating conversation with Xavier concerning some obscure details of eighteenth century theatre, about which he seemed extremely knowledgeable.

There were two on the bus, however, who were none too happy.

Big Mac's stomach was rumbling. He'd been all set for that delicious doughnut! He'd had a taste of the homemade beach plum jam, and it was without a doubt the best filling he'd ever had. And the dough smelled heavenly. "It would have been *so* delicious," he thought sadly.

The other unhappy character was on top of the bus, hanging on by his toenails. He'd almost missed his ride when he had tried (unsuccessfully) to snatch one of the fresh-baked treats. He, too, was pretty sore about the doughnuts. In one day he'd missed two of possibly the best doughnut opportunities in the great state of Massachusetts! And he longed for the nice bed he'd made inside the bus. Sylvanas was fond of his comforts. He wasn't a "rough it" kind of cat.

And worst of all, he still hadn't figured out how to help Hannah. He'd been so certain that the answer was in Boston. And he wasn't so sure about this character Xavier. He said he was ElsBeth's cousin, but Sylvanas wasn't convinced. He seemed too smooth, too unlike Hannah and ElsBeth.

Still, Sylvanas hadn't met any other members of the family except Hannah's husband, Nathaniel, who'd been overcome when trying to keep the peace just before the breakout of the American Civil War in 1860. Even a powerful witch like Nathaniel couldn't ease that much hate.

"Anyway," he thought, "until I know more, I'm not about to trust that fancy-pants Xavier, even if he is distracting Ms. Finch from her habit of picking on ElsBeth. The Finch just can't stand that much spunk," he thought. And being pretty spunky himself, he was sympathetic to ElsBeth's difficulties with the teacher.

ElsBeth just couldn't keep her spunkiness in check. School was difficult for children like that. Particularly when they had a teacher who worshipped authority – her own, that is. It was like oil and water. Sylvanas would have to plan more distractions for ElsBeth's class to keep things in balance between the two. And with the pleasant idea of creating mischief, the oversized cat was able to relax (except for the paw that was holding on tight) and indulge in his favorite activity – he drifted off to sleep.

151

Six Druid Lane

Chapter XXII
HOME SWEET HOME

The high speed ferry back to Hyannis was uneventful, though several of the children did notice a ship sailing erratically on the horizon and wondered if it could be the pirate putting his crew of unseamanlike villains through their paces on the *Bon Adventure*.

Mac drove the bus off the ferry and the children settled into thinking what they'd tell their curious parents about their first field trip off Cape.

ElsBeth advised no lies. "It never pays," she said knowingly. "That doesn't mean you have to tell absolutely *every*thing, though," the little witch added with a twinkle in her eye.

"Yeah," Veronica added. "I'm going to talk about the first part of the trip on the Freedom Trail. It was *very* educational." She rolled her green eyes and started giggling.

"You, on the other hand, may have some more difficult explaining to do," she added to Violet sitting beside her.

"Yeah, I've been thinking about it. There is something fishy about our teacher, Mr. Benedict. When I get back, I'm going to talk to the prince and we'll do some detective work. I somehow think he was in on the kidnapping. I noticed he didn't look at all surprised when it happened. It was almost like he expected it. I'm going to call the school and tell them he gave me permission to stay overnight with you. I bet he won't dare say anything. It's a boarding school, after all, and the last thing they'll want is to tell my parents they lost me for a day! I don't think *I'm* going to be in any trouble at all. I think someone else is," Violet smiled.

Veronica thought that Violet had the makings of a great army general, or maybe a detective, or even a diplomat.

Prince Abu was telling Johnny he'd be honored to stay at his house. He asked if he could call his father, who might have heard something about the kidnapping and might be worried – though he was sure his father trusted him to protect himself. Like Violet, the prince was convinced his teacher was somehow involved in all of this. But he'd have to be skillful in handling the situation. He loved his school and he loved Boston. And if this teacher was a rotten apple, he didn't want to have to leave the school just because of him.

Abu felt sure he could talk this through with his father, whatever came up. He'd even let his father provide him with bodyguards again, if necessary. He hated being looked after as if he couldn't take care of himself, but if it meant he could stay in Boston, in the United States of America, which he had begun to love almost as much as his home, it would be worth it.

Most of all, he wanted to spend time with his new friends on Cape Cod.

As the bus pulled into the school yard, several slightly anxious parents cheered.

"You're back safe and sound!" Veronica's mother hugged her little daughter. "We figured you got caught up in the rush hour traffic, but you were still pretty late."

"Oh, Mom, you worry too much. What could happen on a field trip with Ms. Finch anyway?" she added with a secret smile.

Veronica's mother now noticed Violet, who was standing quietly behind her daughter. Mrs. Smythe crouched down, somewhat confused but friendly, and asked, "Who are you?"

Before Violet could answer, Veronica said, "This is my friend, Violet. I invited her to spend the night. OK, Mom?" she added a little nervously. She had never asked to have a friend over before with no advance notice.

"Well, of course," the young mom replied. "But I should speak with her parents to be sure it's OK with them."

Violet chimed in, "Oh, it's OK, I'm at a boarding school. I just need to talk to my dorm mother and let her know I arrived safely."

"Well, that's fine then." Mrs. Smythe didn't seem to *totally* understand, but the girls were here and safe and happy, and that was the important thing. Veronica's mother smiled and took their hands – the two girls exchanged knowing glances.

On the other side of the parking lot, Frankie's mother greeted him with steaming meatballs and spaghetti. "I just heated it up. A couple of times, actually," she added. "I knew you'd be hungry when you got back from all that hiking around Boston."

"Yeah, all that hiking . . ." And Frankie dug in right there in the school yard.

At the same time, Johnny Twofeathers was introducing Prince Abu to his grandfather, who searched his deep brown almond eyes and accepted the young man

155

immediately. "The prince is welcome always," he said to his grandson.

"Welcome home, Abu," the old man then whispered to the young boy.

Abu hugged him and said, "Yes, my father, I feel I am at one of my true homes." And the two small boys and the tall old man headed off quietly, embraced by the Cape Cod evening.

Lisa was met by her father, who was back from a long research expedition on a vessel owned by the Woods Hole Oceanographic Institute. He had been studying the effects of pollution on the world's seas. "First daughter, I smell the family pet. It seems judgment is lacking, even if the heart is big."

Lisa looked a little ashamed as she climbed into their solar powered, electric vehicle. "Bye, ElsBeth. Trust in family and those you love," she added mysteriously, as she patted her backpack.

One by one the children were met by parents and headed home.

Ms. Finch looked admiringly at Xavier as she waited for the last of the children to leave.

Now there was only ElsBeth, shadowed by an achingly sore Sylvanas.

ElsBeth had said goodbye to all her friends, but somehow she wasn't too anxious to rush home tonight.

She felt she had kind of cheated to go on the trip, and even though her grandmother hadn't outright said, "No," the little witch knew she had taken advantage of her grandmother's recent forgetfulness. Deep down, ElsBeth knew what she'd done was wrong.

She hung her head and started slowly down the road. She knew she would have to face up to her actions. And she decided, right then, she would tell her grandmother the truth. No matter the consequences, she would face them.

And with this resolution, the little witch picked up her pace and felt not so heavy at heart.

Persephone the coyote, following silently beside, also felt more at peace, for she could sense that ElsBeth would now be all right.

Othello the owl noticed the same, and sent out a call so the other local creatures would know that ElsBeth was back safe and sound – in body, mind and spirit.

Bartholomew jumped off the garden stool where he had finally fallen into a restless sleep after worrying about ElsBeth all day. He was so relieved when he heard the news!

And he hopped right over to the porch to meet his young friend.

ElsBeth's little feet crunched along the drive, and Thelonius Chipmunk's smaller feet crunched along beside her. He spoke for all the creatures. "You had us worried, ElsBeth. We're glad you are back."

ElsBeth smiled at the little nutmeg-colored Thelonius and said, "I'm glad I'm back, too. How's Grandmother?" she added anxiously.

Thelonius paused, "Oh, well . . . she's fine . . . she's just the same," he stuttered, and fell back, not wanting to talk more about Hannah Goodspell. That was too upsetting for him to think about.

ElsBeth frowned and looked for the comfort of the moon. She saw his full shining face and felt a little better.

Then a shadow crossed over – a drifting cloud in the shape of that familiar face she'd been seeing the past week or so. It was driving her mad! "Who . . . or what . . . *was* it?"

ElsBeth felt strong hands on her shoulders, but she wasn't afraid. She knew better than to give in to fear. She reached out her heart, and found . . . her cousin.

Of course he was her relation! He'd been trying to contact her for days. The face, the presence! He'd been trying to introduce himself.

"I'm here to help, ElsBeth. I wasn't able to arrive until you were just taking off for Boston, and I thought I'd better follow. I tried to let you know help was on the way over the last week or so, but I'm not sure you know how to interpret those kinds of messages.

"Hannah is sick," he added. "Your grandmother has been on her own for a long time, and even though you are coming along you are not a very skilled witch."

ElsBeth was about to protest when Xavier added kindly, "*Yet*. You are not a very skilled witch *yet*. It is hard to take care of even a small village all by oneself, and the challenges are more difficult every day. You probably noticed it is much cleaner here on the Cape than in Boston."

ElsBeth nodded. For sure she had noticed that.

"Many other witches and I, and even dedicated ordinary people – though how you can call any person 'ordinary' is beyond me – all work very hard to fix the terrible damage being done when we pollute the environment. The planet is sick, and even the beautiful places like the Cape, where people have really tried to protect the environment, are in need of help. And magic

158

alone just isn't enough to fix things now. It will take both magic and science, and a lot of caring people and witches working hard together, to make things better."

ElsBeth couldn't help remembering what Captain Thomas Jacques had said to Robert Hillman-Jones. About really caring and fighting for something that was important. *That* made life interesting and fun. And an adventure worth sharing with friends! And *this*, ElsBeth thought, was the real *Legend of the Pirate*.

For her, this meant fighting to help the planet be healthy and safe, for all her friends and the creatures who live here. And this was kind of like fighting for freedom that the captain had done back in the 1700's.

ElsBeth was glad she had met Captain Thomas Jacques. And she knew she would always remember him.

Xavier continued, "All the things that have been happening around town are because your grandmother has lost the full control of her magic. Hannah just hasn't been able to concentrate and keep up. She is still a powerful witch. But she's been alone too long and this has stretched her magic too thin. It hasn't really been the fairies at all.

"We can make her well. You and I together. Sometimes it takes more than one. And with the planet in this much of a mess, it will take us all. Will you help?"

ElsBeth turned around and hugged Xavier as tight as she could, tears streaming down her face. "Of course, I'll help," she choked out.

After the long overdue hug, the two began to glow.

And as they continued down the drive, Sylvanas stepped up with them. Persephone the coyote followed, as did Thaddeus Crane and Thelonius Chipmunk. And finally Bartholomew joined them as they reached the bottom step of the porch.

The odd little group stepped onto the porch just as Hannah opened the kitchen door to greet them.

"ElsBeth, you're home! I made you some oatmeal bread and we have fresh butter from Farmer Green's cow, Beatrice." Hannah went on, not focused, and not really seeing ElsBeth or the others, as if in a dream.

"Hannah," Xavier's eyes shone with tears. "You have help, we are here. It's OK."

The handsome Xavier folded the little old witch in his arms. ElsBeth grabbed onto her grandmother, too. And all the animals nuzzled up to the three witches. Anyone watching would have seen a soft, warm light begin to shine from the porch at Six Druid Lane.

Hannah still looked befuddled, but she was smiling a contented little smile. Then suddenly the air was disturbed. There was a smell of ozone, and the two fairies swung in near to Hannah's head.

"Wake up, you foolish old witch!" they said, impatient as always. "Can't you see they love you? Can't you see they need you? We *all* need you! Wake up!

"You have work to do, and you've been falling down on the job. Get it together!" The beautiful little rosebud lips chattered away.

Finally the female fairy, the most impatient one, gave the old witch a firm pinch!

"Ouch, you stop that, you little pest!" Hannah's old voice broke out in protest. And then she said, "My, how nice to see everyone," as she finally noticed all who were gathered on the porch.

Then her eyes focused on Xavier.

"Xavier, is it really you?"

"Yes. It really is."

Hannah laughed. "I feel like I've been gone away for a long time and I'm finally back home. And here you all are! Come in, come in! You are all welcome!"

The fairies went first, pushing everyone out of the way as they rushed to the table. They hadn't had a witch's home cooking for ages!

And over the threshold followed the others – ElsBeth beaming as wide as could be, Xavier happy to be able to help his favorite aunt at last, and Bartholomew and all the rest – relieved to know that things were going to begin to get better again.

Last through the door was a very happy, very large black cat.

"I'm glad I finally solved that situation," Sylvanas said to himself. Then added loudly, grinning ear to ear, "What did you say was for dinner?"

And everyone laughed.

THE END

Author's Note

Captain Thomas Jacques – and the notorious pirate Billy Bowlegs mentioned in *The Cape Cod Witch and the Pirate's Treasure* – both have a basis in real characters. Billy Bowleg's life parallels Captain William Kidd, and Captain Thomas Jacques shares his life's story with Captain Thomas Jacques Grouchy.

Captain Kidd, who lived about one hundred years before Grouchy, is reputed to have buried a treasure on Cape Cod, which is still searched for today, and to have had a lady friend on the Cape, too – just like in the first book of the *Cape Cod Witch Series*. And Captain Grouchy did steal and donate lovely carved angels to the Old North Church in Boston, where he was popular and warmly regarded. And he was, in fact, a revolutionary in the late 1700's.

Both Grouchy and Kidd also felt wrongly accused of being "pirates" and passionately proclaimed they were patriotic "privateers". Whether they were misunderstood and unjustly accused, or not, they are part of Cape Cod's rich sea-faring history and legend.

Double-Double Chocolate Chip Fairy-Cream Cupcakes

(ElsBeth's Favorite!)

From Hannah Goodspell's Secret Recipe Book

14 tablespoons butter (best from Farmer Green's cow, Beatrice)
½ cup unsweetened cocoa
1¼ cups agave nectar
3 large eggs (ElsBeth and Hannah like Hattie the Hen's eggs best)
2 teaspoons vanilla extract
½ cup whole wheat pastry flour
1 pinch of salt
1 cup walnuts – chopped (optional)
½ cup chocolate chips (ElsBeth likes the grain-sweetened ones.)

1. Place oven rack in the middle of the oven. Preheat oven to 375 degrees.
2. Line 12-count muffin tin with cupcake liners.
3. Melt butter. Whisk in unsweetened cocoa. Add agave nectar and mix well.
4. In another bowl lightly beat together eggs with vanilla extract. Add egg mixture to the cocoa mixture and blend together. Then mix in flour and salt. Fold in walnuts and chocolate chips.
5. Pour into muffin tins and bake for about 20 minutes. To test for doneness, insert a wooden toothpick into the center of cupcake; the toothpick should have some moist crumbs attached to it. Do not over bake!
6. Remove from the oven and cool completely on a wire rack.

Fairy-Cream

1 cup heavy cream (also best from Beatrice)
¼ cup agave nectar, more or less
1 teaspoon vanilla

Beat cream until stiff (hint: sprinkle unflavored gelatin on the cream as you beat it and it will become stiff more easily and hold its shape longer). Then slowly add agave nectar and vanilla. (Hannah lets ElsBeth lick the bowl.) Then place a cupcake in a pretty dish, and add as much fairy cream as you like.

And remember, it is always the most fun to share!

ACKNOWLEDGEMENT

We want to relay a special thank
you to Bill Hiss of Bates College.
We appreciate and are fortunate he
spared the time to edit this book
and the earlier ElsBeth adventure.

Any errors, however, be assured are
the responsibility of the author alone.

We also want to send special thanks to
Beth, a docent at the Old North Church
in Boston, who led the author on a
personal tour of the crypt beneath the
church and explained its rich history.

ElsBeth's Further Adventures

Things are again hopeful in the small Cape village. And life goes on. But what sort of adventure or trouble will the little witch and her special friends find next?

There are rumors of a trip out West. The gazing ball shows a haunted gold mine and restless Indian spirits. And still that Scottish castle flickers in and out.

Sylvanas knows that Hannah Goodspell plans to give ElsBeth a special present. Will it be her coveted cookbook, handed down these many generations, containing the family's magically delicious favorite recipes?

We will have to watch carefully to find out!

And if you haven't yet read it, be sure to catch up with ElsBeth and Sylvanas and all their friends in the daring story of *The Cape Cod Witch and the Pirate's Treasure!*

Visit www.capecodlittlewitch.com to find out more.

The Cape Cod Witch
~ and the ~
Pirate's Treasure

Illustrator and Author

In *The Cape Cod Witch Series*, the author calls upon her family's long history in New England, including a Revolutionary "Green Mountain Boy," Cape Cod cranberry farmers and artists, and an oft-told family legend that as her grandmother's ancestors stepped off the *Mayflower*, her grandfather's relatives were there to greet them. With a degree in Environmental Science, Palmer weaves in her stories a message of care for our precious natural resources and the environment.

The author welcomes readers' comments and may be contacted at author@capecodlittlewitch.com

Illustrator Melanie Therrien lives in western Maine with her husband Glenn, stepson Dylon, their dogs Sophie and Tito, as well as their three cats, one of which was the model for Sylvanas in the ElsBeth books. The juried fine artist looks to the state's natural beauty for inspiration for her fanciful images and landscapes. Therrien enjoys creating imaginary worlds and interesting characters in her preferred medium of acrylics. The stylistic artwork for *The Cape Cod Witch Series* is her first book illustration project.

The artist may be contacted at therrien6@myfairpoint.net or visit her website www.wickedillustrations.com

Printing by

Cape Cod National Offset & Bindery, Inc.
11 Jonathan Bourne Drive, Unit 3
Pocasset, MA 02559
Contact: Paul Petrie, Account Executive/Estimator
Tel: 508-563-5001 / Fax: 508-563-5002
paul.ccnationaloffset@comcast.net
www.capecodnationaloffset.com